TO JEAN,
THANK YOU FOR COMING
TONIGHT. I TRUST YOU
WILL ENJOY "TWISTED OBSESSION".
TAKE CARE & "STAY SAFE"
- MARK

National Praise for Mark Kearney and Twisted Obsession

"A very dark and scary ride to a place most of us will never see. Mark Kearney's book is reminiscent of Jim Thompson's classic The Killer Inside Me and may, in fact, signal the beginning of a new chapter in crime fiction: Virginia Noir. Read it."

Peter Blauner
New York Times bestselling author of *"The Intruder* and *Slipping Into Darkness"*

"Twisted Obsession is Mark Kearney's first novel and we can only hope it will not be his last. . ."

"This suspense novel is a real page turner that leaves you wanting more. Hopefully Kearney won't disappoint and we can look forward to a sequel in the near future."

Teresa Gilliam
Assistant Library Director,
Waynesboro, VA

"One of the scariest books I have ever read. Mark Kearney managed something no one has in a long time, he creeped me out. Not a bad thing, I just thought I was more jaded than that."

Darla Cook is the Assistant for NY Times # 1 best selling author Laurell K. Hamilton.

TWISTED OBSESSION

By

Mark Kearney

Realm of Insanity Press

This is a work of fiction. Names, characters, places, and incidents either are the product of the author's imagination or are used fictitiously, and any resemblance to actual persons, living or dead, business establishments, events, or locales is entirely coincidental.

Copyright © 2007 by Mark Kearney
Text design by Lauren Ferrell
Cover design © 2007 by Lauren Ferrell
Cover Photo © 2007 iStock.com/GerMan101 - Jan Bruder

All rights reserved. No part of this book may be used or reproduced in any form or by any means, or stored in a database or retrieval system, without prior written permission of the publisher except in the case of brief quotations embodied in critical articles and reviews.

First Edition 2007

10 Digit ISBN 0-9794998-2-8
13 Digit ISBN 978-0-9794998-2-1

Library of Congress Cataloging-in-Publication Data

Kearney, Mark.
Twisted obsession / by Mark Kearney. -- 1st ed.
p. cm.
ISBN 978-0-9794998-3-8 (hardcopy : acid-free paper) -- ISBN 978-0-9794998-2-1 (pbk. : acid-free paper)
1. Police brutality--Fiction. 2. Virginia--Fiction. I. Title.
PS3611.E18T85 2007
813'.6--dc22
2007022106

Realm of Insanity Press
P O Box 3285
Chester, VA 23831
www.realmofinsanitypress.com

Printed on acid-free paper in the United States of America

Acknowledgements

There are many people who helped me during the process of making this book. My appreciation goes out to all of you mentioned and to many others who have helped me in various other ways.

 Laura Maine helped me from day one all the way through to the end. Thank you.

Author and the co-founder of The Book 'Em Foundation, p.m. terrell for the feedback you gave me early on.

Tina Norcross, for being a friend and helping me so often with the support you give me for my literacy programs, especially on those days when I wonder am I really doing any good or not. Thank you.

Author Linda Morelli, Author and friend Lauren Ferrell, and Author Carisa Star

Movie Producer Anne Marie Gillen

Chief Doug Davis of the Waynesboro Police Department, even though I hope you aren't disappointed in Jay and how he turned out.

Captain Mike Martin, Waynesboro Police Department, for telling me to think outside the box several years ago. That ultimately led to where I am today.

My editor, Bobbie Christmas,

And of course, it goes without saying, but I'll still say it, my deepest appreciation goes to Sonia, Zack and Alex for all they do for me.

*D*edication

I'd like to dedicate this book to my friend, Laura Maine. I couldn't have done it without you. And, it goes without saying; I owe a tremendous amount to my family. Thank you all for supporting me in my writing. I greatly appreciate it.

Author Note

So, I ask myself, why would a man who is out to positively impact the world through The Book 'Em Foundation and his literacy programs write a book where he created an evil character who hopefully will never exist on this planet?

There are several reasons. The easy answer is to say that it is the story that came out of me. I sat down one summer day to try my hand at writing, not knowing what I would write, and the first chapter of Twisted Obsession is what came out. I didn't plan this book out and many nights, I had no idea how a chapter would end until I got to the ending.

However, there is more to it than that.

I am on this earth to positively impact others. Yet, through my time in the military, my time as a police officer and just my time in life, I have found there is still evil in this world. I have also seen where a segment of our population is still naïve to the problems that are out there.

Dear reader, my hope is my character Jay will scare you, will terrify you with his actions, and also wake you up to the potential evil out there. Do I think a Jay really exists on this earth? Well, I don't think so and I sure hope not.

However, does this world have drugs that will rot a person? Yes, meth is one of those drugs and it's in your neighborhood.

Are gang members alive and well in small towns across this country? Yes, they are.

Are terrorists who will strap a bomb to themselves and walk into a crowd of innocent people inside our borders? Probably so.

Jay is a fictional character created from my mind. I based him on no person that I have known or hopefully will ever know.

Yet, when I look around me, I see things in this world that scare me much more than Jay does.

I do hope you enjoy Twisted Obsession. Scare yourself by reading novels. At the same time, try to do your part to improve this world in some positive way. Working together, all of us can and will make this world a better place.

I'll wrap this note up with one of my favorite sayings. Keep smiling, as smiles help the world to continue spinning in a positive direction.

Mark Kearney 3/17/07

CHAPTER 1

A bullet whizzing by really does sound like the crack of thunder.

Jay leaned against the police cruiser, gun poised for action as the thought quickly flashed through his mind. Why the hell did I become a policeman in the first place?

There was a pleasant scent of burning firewood in the crisp autumn air, and he detected the faint aroma of burning leaves. A wispy column of smoke curled upwards from the ramshackle house. Its tentacles circled around the chimney in the brisk wind, as he aimed his gun.

He had called for backup immediately following the first shot and now sirens wailed in the distance. Thank God, the Cavalry is coming. Jay wiped a bead of sweat from his brow.

Crack! Crack! Two rapid shots fired in succession. Jay leaned forward and caught a glimpse of movement from behind the corner of the two-story brick house. A blur of red and black plaid, all jumbled together like a jigsaw puzzle. Only he didn't have the pieces put together.

He couldn't believe he had been stupid enough to walk into this situation. The call had come out as a domestic with weapons involved. Jay had only been a block away, so he had arrived within seconds. A working class, residential area, and the houses were fairly close together.

This neighborhood had its share of calls over the years, but normally they were minor in nature. The department received the occasional domestic, but more often than not it was some vandalism or a petty larceny. He had never expected to get shot at, but still, there's always a first time.

Jay wasn't the best shot, but he knew how to shoot and he'd always told himself that he would do his best to kill anyone who was trying to kill him. The red and black he had glimpsed was the plaid shirt of the perp. He saw it again, between the corner of the house and a still-green bush. Then, hysterical screams from deep in the bowels of the house reached his ears, causing his blood to boil and his ears to burn.

Slowly the screams subsided into a resigned cry and Jay didn't know what was worse: the screams that demanded he rescue the hostage, or the whimper of a woman prepared to accept her fate.

Crack! Crack! Crack! One of the three shots

skipped off the hood of his blue and white cruiser, a Crown Victoria. That bullet came too close for comfort. Jay glanced at the house, and spotted the same portion of the plaid shirt. Just the briefest glimpse; a hand pulling back with a smoking pistol in it. Without hesitation, he took careful aim and slowly squeezed the trigger. The person jumped and screamed in pain and a thin, white male came stumbling out with the pistol still in his hand.

Jay yelled, "Drop the gun, drop the gun!" The suspect raised his arm and started taking aim. Jay fired. He fired as he'd been taught to do, without hesitation, without thinking, without feeling. Just the automatic movement of his forefinger pressing against the trigger, again, and again and again...

The tension in his neck amplified, his veins throbbed, his pulse pounded. He could still hear screams from deep within the house as he kept firing until he heard nothing but the unmistakable click that signified an empty chamber and magazine.

Uniformed and plain-clothes cops arrived as Jay ran toward the suspect, who now lay face down in the grass. He stopped short and watched as the cops rushed from their cars. Relief filled him, though he could feel his heart pounding and his adrenalin rushing through his veins. Then, everything slowed down, became almost slow motion.

Brent, another officer on his shift, arrived on scene, glanced in his direction, and then immediately headed his way. He stopped for a second to speak with another officer. Brent had worked on Jay's shift for about six months now. Slender with long legs, he was younger than Jay and had only been a cop for two years. As he strode across the yard, a serious look replaced his normally smiling face.

"What happened, man?"

Jay took several deep breaths, trying to calm himself. "I'm not sure. You know me; I don't like to wait for back up. Soon as I got out of my car, someone started shooting."

"He's dead, you know. You hit him several times in the chest. How many times did you shoot him?"

"I don't remember," Jay said. "I shot him once and he came out waving his gun as if he was going to shoot at me again. I just started pulling the trigger. Shit, I killed a guy and you know we've all talked about what if something like this happens. What do you think the Department will do? Will they stand behind me or will they let me get hung out to dry?"

Eli Thompson, the ranking officer on the scene, trudged over to Jay. "How you doing?"

Jay swallowed down the anxiety that had lodged in his throat. "Okay, I guess."

"Here." Thompson took out his Glock and handed it to Jay. "Give me yours."

Jay knew it was normal departmental policy for the supervisor to take possession of the gun of an officer who has been involved in a shooting. It was also normal for that supervisor to give the officer his own gun, as long as they thought the shooting was justified.

"Eli, what's going to happen to me?" asked Jay.

"From the looks of things, I don't think you have anything to worry about."

"Yeah, that's easy for you to say." Jay tucked the gun into his holster. "It's not your butt on the line."

Eli met his gaze head on. "From what I'm hearing, you were completely justified."

Brent spoke up. "Who's doing the investigation?"

"Dave is."

"Good."

"Anyway," Eli returned his attention to Jay, "we need to head back to the Police Department so he can get your statement. He'll be along in a few minutes, once he's finished talking with a couple next door. They pretty much saw everything from their upstairs window. According to what I'm hearing . . ."

"What did the couple say? Did they see him shooting at me first?" Jay's voice rose to a higher, excited pitch as he completed the question.

"Yes, they saw him shoot at you first. You were completely justified in what you did." He placed his hand on Jay's shoulder and led him toward the cruiser. "Let's go to the PD and let these guys take care of the scene. Dave is going to meet us down there. He'll get your side of things, but then I want you to go home."

Dave was one of the detectives in the department. He and Jay had gone through the Basic Academy together and they knew each other pretty well. Both had gotten busy with their jobs and families, but they still liked to sit and catch each other up on life's happenings from time to time.

Eli and Jay went back a long ways as well. Jay had been hired a little over sixteen years ago and, at that time, Eli was not even a Corporal. He had only been in the Police Department about a year himself. Eli was the one who taught him how to shoot and they had been buddies ever since. Eli was one of those guys that everyone got along with and it didn't hurt that he was sharp as a tack. That was one of the reasons that he had made rank so quickly. He also knew what he was doing and Jay believed it wouldn't be too much longer until Eli Thompson was made Chief of Police.

Now, Jay didn't know what was going to happen with his career. He had already been having thoughts about making a career change, but what impact would shooting and killing one of the local toads have on him?

Eli talked non-stop all the way to the Police Department. Just friendly chatter, but it kept the tension out of the air. Once there, Eli got him a cup of black coffee and let him sit in his sparsely furnished office while they waited for Dave to arrive. Jay stared at Eli's walnut finished desk, his mind on his uncertain future. There were several pictures on the walls of Eli and other members of his SWAT Team.

Eli was a large man. He stood about 6'4" and was 235 pounds of solid muscle. He had made the SWAT team early in his career and now was in charge of the team.

Dave got there within a few minutes and immediately said, "That was some good shooting, Jay, but why did you shoot so many times?"

Jay hesitantly answered him. "I don't know. I've always told myself if I ever had to pull the trigger, I was going to keep pulling it until I knew the suspect was down."

"Well, from what I can tell, you were completely justified in shooting Moe."

"Moe? Was it Moe Jackson that I shot?" asked Jay.

Dave raised an eyebrow. "Yes, didn't you know?"

"No, I never saw him close enough to tell who it was. After he went down and I got closer, I saw he was lying face down. All I knew then was that he was a white guy with long, dirty blond hair, a red and black plaid flannel shirt and blue jeans. Then, everyone arrived and I backed away before they turned the body over."

Jay related to Dave the events that had transpired. After arriving, he had marked 10-23, which meant he was on location. Jay had gotten out of his cruiser and started walking around it, when he'd heard the first shot. When he had heard several more shots, he'd immediately taken cover behind his cruiser.

Jay told him about getting a glimpse of the shooter, being able to take that first shot – the one that hit him and brought the man out into the open. Jay saw Moe raise his gun up again, repeatedly yelled at him to drop the gun, but Jay knew he would have to shoot again. That was when he started shooting and the next thing he knew, it was over. The man was down.

"Thanks, Jay. That pretty much matches up with what Trixie told us." Trixie was Moe's off-and-on girlfriend. The two of them had a love-hate relationship. Pretty much every cop on the force knew both of them, for they had many domestics and other problems over the past five years or so.

Jay released a sigh of relief. "What about the couple next door?"

Dave stood, "They told us basically the same thing you and Trixie did. Don't worry, buddy."

"So, what happens now?"

Eli's face broke into a grin as he said, "You get a few days off with pay while the State Police come in."

"Hey, something good does come out of all of this. Time off with pay, what more can a guy ask for? It doesn't count as vacation time, does it?" asked Jay sarcastically.

"Always looking for some time off, aren't you? Well, you got some, but don't get too used to it. I have a feeling you'll be back to work in two or three days." Eli stood. "Now get out of here and go home to that wife and those two kids of yours."

Together, Eli and Jay walked out of the PD and to Jay's car.

Jay thought they were relatively calm after one of their officers had killed someone but, after thinking on that for a second, he realized it was a normal reaction. Cops, firefighters and rescue workers always joked with each other more than normal when they were around hurt or injured people, or even a death from a car accident. It was a defense mechanism and anyone who worked in public service realized that fact.

"Thanks, man," Jay said, shaking Eli's hand.

"You taught me how to shoot when I got hired, and for that I owe you a lot. Perhaps my life."

"I'm glad you're okay, Jay," he replied. "I know it probably sucks to know you killed a person, but you did good. Shit happens, but we have a job to do."

"Yeah, I know. I remember back in the academy when some instructor told us it was better to be judged by twelve than to be carried by six. I've always kept that in the back of my mind."

"Go home, Jay. Call me if you need anything. Tell Angela I said hi and give the kids a hug for me. How old are they now?"

"Tim just turned thirteen and Marie is eight. I'm not sure how I'm going to tell them I shot and killed a person, but I have to. They'll find out soon enough once the media gets a hold of this," Jay said.

"Yeah, good luck with that. I don't think you have to worry about the media blowing this out of proportion or anything. I'm sure the other kids in school may get on them, but hopefully it'll all die down fairly quick."

"I just hope the State Police agree with everything you are saying. You know as well as I do this could be my career if they don't. Or, even worse, Moe's family may decide to sue me."

Eli laughed, but the look in his eyes held no humor. "Yeah, you have that right. His family will probably try to sue you. Don't worry, the State Police will clear you and the PD will stand behind you one hundred percent."

"Thanks, Eli, for everything".

As Jay drove away, he thought about what had

transpired that day. He had taken another human's life. He knew his life was going to be different from here on out, but he didn't know how.

CHAPTER 2

When Jay arrived back at his house, he noticed the pile of leaves under his maple tree that needed raking. He walked up the sidewalk, through the leaves, to the front door of his house. It was a white, two-story Cape Cod style house. He unlocked the door and walked into the quiet and empty house. It seemed so eerie to him after all of the excitement of the past several hours.

Jay slowly walked around the house. He went through the kitchen, into the hallway and then the living room. There were many photographs of him and his family spread throughout the house. In the living room, above the fireplace, there were several shots of Tim playing baseball and Marie playing soccer. His favorite picture was of him and Angela that had been taken prior to Tim being born. He was a lot younger with longer hair and a goatee.

Jay looked in the refrigerator and behind the milk and orange juice; he saw a single 12-ounce bottle of Moosehead beer. Normally, he would wait until the evening when the kids were in bed to have a beer or two. He decided that maybe he needed to drink it now.

Angela and the kids arrived home just as he finished the bottle. Angela quickly walked into the house. The kids stayed outside playing. Angela looked tired, but still quite pretty dressed in a pair of brown slacks and a black sweater over her blouse. She was surprised to see him, as he normally didn't get home until eight o'clock after working a 12-hour day shift.

"Hon, what are you doing home so early? Why are you drinking?" She looked closely at him. "What's wrong?"

"I have some bad news."

"What's wrong, Jay? Is it your brother?" she asked, her brow furrowing in concern.

Jay's brother was only three years older, but he had been diagnosed with lung cancer a year ago. Twenty years of smoking non-filtered Camels had taken its toll on him.

"No... I killed a person today."

"Oh, my God. Are you okay? Are you in trouble?"

"I'm fine. It's just weird to know I've killed a person. It was justified and I'm not in any trouble, but they have to do a routine investigation and I get to stay home for a few days while they do it," Jay said as he smiled faintly.

The house was silent for a minute as the couple stood there in the kitchen. The dishes were piled on the counter from the morning's breakfast. The kids were still out in the front yard and their playful shouts could be heard even with the windows closed.

"Are you sure you're okay?"

"Yes."

"Who was it?"

"It was Moe Jackson."

"Who's he?"

"One of the local toads we've all dealt with for several years now. He was shooting at me and I had to do it. I just had to. There was no way around it."

"Are you going to tell the kids?"

"I have to. You know how it is when a cop kills someone. It always makes the news, usually around the entire state and sometimes the country. At least he was a white guy and they won't be crying that I'm a racist. I'm so glad for that. I have to tell the kids, but there is no need to tell them too much."

"I agree. But let's tell them together."

The kids took it okay. Tim was into guns and was at the age where he thought it was cool that his father was a cop. He actually said it was kind of cool Jay had shot a man and he said he wanted to call his best friend Matthew to tell him. Angela talked him out of doing that.

Marie didn't really say too much or have much of a reaction. She was only eight and still pretty young. However she was frowning slightly and her eyes were downcast, as if she was saddened by what she had been told.

A few hours later, after the kids were in bed, Angela and Jay sat in the living room talking about the day's event. Jay explained in detail about the shooting. He told her Moe had been shooting at him and when he was able to take a shot, he took advantage of it.

"Once he got out in the open after I hit him the first time and he started taking aim at me, it was almost like I lost control. I just kept shooting and shooting. Even at the range, we never shoot our entire magazine at once, but I emptied all sixteen shots. I still remember the smell and seeing the smoke curling out of the end of the barrel.

"I can still see him falling. He landed in the grass and didn't move at all. I knew he was dead once I got close to him. There was blood seeping out from under his body and he wasn't moving."

That night, Jay slept fairly well. The next morning was a typical morning with Angela getting ready for work and getting the kids ready for school. Jay got up and went out to get the paper first thing with a cup of black coffee in hand.

There it was. Right on the front page of the newspaper, **"Police Officer Shoots and Kills Armed Suspect."** The article was fairly factual and portrayed Jay in a positive light. It mentioned the awards he had received over the years and how he had never been in any trouble.

After Angela left with the kids, Jay read over the article several more times. There was a picture of him there as well, taken a few years earlier.

Eli was even quoted as saying that Jay had taken appropriate action for the situation. Good ol' Eli. He'll help me out any way he can, thought Jay.

As the day progressed, Jay kept thinking about the shooting. It was like watching a re-run of a movie, seeing the same scene over and over. Nothing ever changed, and if anything, the vision got clearer each time he replayed it in his mind.

Moe Jackson deserved to die. What did he expect after opening fire on a police officer? I did society a favor by shooting that SOB. Once Jay got that thought in his mind, he couldn't get rid of it.

Around lunchtime, Jay decided to go to the local store to pick up a six-pack. He got into his blue Ford F-250 and drove the two miles to get there. Fall had arrived early and he saw smoke spiraling out of several chimneys. Halloween is just a few days away and I bet it's going to be a cold one, he thought.

While walking through Food Lion, an older gentleman approached him. The white haired, bearded guy told him he had done the right thing. "There are too many of these punk kids around here who have no respect for us good, decent people. The world is better off without him. I know you don't get many thanks for the job you do, but I'm thanking you. I couldn't do it, but I'm glad that you're there for us."

While Jay paid for the six-pack of Fosters Lager in bottles, the cashier gave him a funny look. She had asked for his ID, as the sign said anyone under 40 should expect to get carded. When she saw his name, she looked up and Jay could see anger in her blue eyes.

She didn't say anything, but she shoved his change at him and gave him a dirty look as he was walking out.

Well, fuck her too, he thought. Moe deserved to die and I did what I had to.

CHAPTER 3

Back in his own living room, Jay cracked open a brown bottle of Fosters and flipped on the TV. There he was, right on the first channel he came to. He watched as a local reporter gave background on his stellar career. Not a lot was said about Moe, except for his numerous arrests and past trouble with the police.

Jay took several telephone calls during the day. Several of his buddies at the PD called just to check up on him to see how he was doing. Eli called him twice, just to let him know what the State Police were saying. They kept saying it was justified. Eli told Jay he would be back to work in another day or two, if he was ready to come back.

"Hell, yeah, I'm ready to come back. Just tell me when, and I'll be there."

However, Jay felt strange and the feeling got stronger as the day progressed. Jay felt his emotions changing several times. He was justified in shooting Moe. But, why, why, did Moe start shooting at him? Poor SOB, he was probably smoking meth and didn't know what he was doing. At least the world is rid of Moe and it's a better place without him being here.

It was the next day when Eli called him and said the State Police had closed the case. It was a justified shooting. Jay could come back to work the following day, if he wanted.

"All right, Eli. I'll be there bright and early and better than ever."

"Jay, just take your time. If you want to stay home for a couple more days, that's okay. I'll work it out. You just went through a traumatic experience. There's no need to rush right back to work. Stay home another day or two or even a week. You deserve it."

"I don't know, Eli. You know the old saying about when someone falls off a horse; they need to get right back on. I feel like I need to get back to work as soon as I can, but I'll listen to what you tell me."

That evening, when Angela got home, Jay met her at the door. Angela was there without the kids, as she had called saying she was going to drop them off at her mother's house. They were going to stay there for several days. She gave him a huge hug when she saw him, but almost immediately backed away saying, "How much have you had to drink today?"

"I bought a six-pack and I drank it all."

Angela got a soft look in her eyes and gave Jay another hug. She asked him if he wanted to talk about what had happened.

"It's just a weird feeling to know that I took another person's life. I still feel I did the right thing and I would do it again, but it hit me today that I met Moe's parents a year or two earlier on a call. They seemed like good, decent people. How do they feel now about what happened?"

"Honey, I'm sure they're sad about Moe's death. But if they're good, decent people, then they will know you did what you had to do."

Jay heaved a big sigh and agreed with her.

Angela gave him a soft kiss on his lips and started rubbing his shoulders. "The kids aren't here. Do you want to go up to the bedroom?"

He really wasn't in the mood to make love, but Jay followed her up the steps to their bedroom.

Jay didn't feel the greatest afterwards. It just wasn't enjoyable to him making love with his wife tonight and that was a first for him.

He thought that Angela probably picked up on his feelings, but she didn't say anything. Normally, she was quite talkative when they finished. However, tonight, she was looking strangely at him and staying silent.

That night, Jay had trouble falling asleep. He got out of his king-sized bed and made his way to the living room. He turned the boob tube on, but sat there flipping through channels without finding anything good to watch. He turned the TV back off and turned the radio on.

Tim must have left it tuned to a rap station. Jay leaned back to listen. The music got his heart pumping due to the fast beat. Then the first song ended and the next one came on.

Jay had trouble understanding all of it, but he picked out words like "Kill the Cop, Shoot the Mother Fucking Cops."

What is this shit, Jay thought? He got up and changed the station to a local country station. Country music was probably his favorite type to listen to. At least in country music they only sang about lost loves and getting drunk, not killing cops.

Jay sat there for a long time, staring off into space, thinking about all that had happened. The impact of taking another human's life had hit him and he wasn't sure what to think.

He kept telling himself he was justified in what he did. He had been cleared by the State Police and could go back to work if he wanted to. However, each time he thought he'd convinced himself he would be okay, he would get a mental image of Moe's mother. That stopped his thought process in its tracks.

What was wrong with him? Why did he keep thinking about this? Earlier in the day, when the Chief had called him, he had suggested that Jay should probably talk to the PD's Psychologist. The Chief had said no matter how he was feeling at the moment, it would be a good idea to do so.

Maybe he should do as the Chief suggested and go talk to the PD's Psychologist about this. He told himself he would call in the morning to set up an appointment. Jay also decided he would take one, maybe two days off before he went back to work.

Finally, pushing 3AM, Jay went back to the bedroom and climbed into bed. Angela stirred and mumbled, "Are you okay?"

"I'm fine, I just wasn't tired. Good night."

Angela was already back asleep. Jay looked at her in the light from the bathroom and thought how beautiful she looked, especially when she was sleeping. He kissed her softly on the cheek and then rolled over and tried to doze off.

When Angela's alarm clock buzzed at 6AM, Jay reached across Angela and turned it off. He didn't know if he'd slept any or not. It seemed he had just lain there for the past several hours, thinking about Moe and the shooting.

When Jay finally climbed out of bed and meandered his way to the kitchen, Angela was making breakfast. He smelled the aroma of coffee in the air mixed with a smell of bacon and eggs.

"Honey, did you sleep any last night? You have dark bags under your eyes. I've never seen you like this before."

"I don't think I slept at all. I just kept thinking about the shooting. Did I really have to shoot him? I could've waited for back up. Maybe we could have talked him into dropping the gun, coming out into the open... maybe nobody would've died."

"Come on, Jay. Don't do this to yourself. You had a job to do and you did it. Honey, you are a great cop. You did the right thing. Don't second-guess yourself about this. You'll just beat yourself up if you do. Don't do that."

Jay looked at her with his steely brown eyes. He knew she loved him, but he felt distant from her. It pained him to feel this way. They had a long and happy marriage. He was careful not to say anything. Knowing him, he would say it the wrong way and upset his wife.

"Honey, come on," Angela was saying. "Eat some breakfast. Then go back to bed and get some sleep."

"Okay." Jay poked at his bacon and eggs, but he didn't eat much. The phone rang, startling him into dropping his fork on the floor. Angela answered it. She talked for several minutes. He picked up that she was talking to her mother about the kids.

After a minute or two, Angela hung up the phone. She said her mother had told her Marie woke up crying several times in the night, with bad dreams.

"Marie never wakes up. This shooting must have affected her more than we thought," Angela said.

"She's a tough kid. In a few days she'll be fine." Jay said it with more conviction than he felt. He wasn't going to tell Angela, but he didn't think *he* was fine anymore with this mess.

Angela left for work a little bit later. At 9AM Jay called to make an appointment with the PD's Psychologist. He found out that Doc Miller was out of town on vacation. They told him he could see another doctor, but Jay knew Doc Miller and liked him, so he made an appointment for a morning after he had returned.

Jay walked outside and picked up the day's newspaper. He saw a smaller article, still on the front page, but not quite as big and bold as yesterday's article. Well, he thought, maybe in a few days this'll all die down and life can get back to normal.

CHAPTER 4

It was 1PM, and Jay was back home after a quick trip to the grocery store. It was a sunny, but chilly day outside. Jay tuned into a country radio station and the song playing was the Big and Rich song about riding a horse and saving a cowboy. Wow, what a song to crack his first beer open on. Jay had bought a twelve-pack earlier in the morning and as he sipped his first one, he wondered if life would ever get back to normal.

All morning, except for his quick trip to Food Lion, he'd watched TV or paced around the house. Once again, it was all Moe in his mind. Moe and guns, bullets and blood. Why do I keep thinking about this crap? Jay thought.

Eli stopped by his house around 2PM. He commented on the beer Jay was drinking, but didn't really say too much about it. Eli was a fairly heavy drinker and Jay didn't think he found it unusual for anyone to be drinking a beer in the afternoon when they were off from work.

"I just wanted to return your gun to you. You know the Virginia State Police cleared you. You can come back to work whenever you want to. You have time on the books, so take a week or two off if you want."

"Thanks, Eli. I'll probably stay off the rest of the week, but I'll be back to work on Monday. A couple more days off, then the weekend and I'll be good as new."

"That's fine, Jay," Eli said as he patted him on the back. "Call me if you need anything."

Eli left a few minutes later. Jay stood in the doorway watching him pull out of the driveway. There was a cool breeze blowing and the scent of fall was in the air. He would have to get out and rake some leaves soon, but not today.

Jay got another beer and sat on the patio. He was wearing a Baltimore Orioles sweatshirt and an old pair of jeans, but he was still chilly. After a few minutes, he went inside and got a ball cap to put on.

He sat on the back deck for a while, sipping his beer and thinking. He watched the leaves twirl around in a circle like mini tornadoes. On the next trip into the house to use the bathroom, Jay grabbed his small cooler and put ice and several beers in it. That way, he wouldn't have to constantly get up and go back inside whenever he wanted another one.

Even though they lived in the city, Jay had almost two acres of land with woods full of oaks, locusts and maple trees bordering his property. There were always plenty of deer, squirrels, rabbits, groundhogs and all kinds of birds. As he sat there drinking, he saw three deer walk into and then out of his yard.

Squirrels were all over the place, running around like little fanatics trying to find all of the acorns to bury around the yard. Stupid animals, he thought. They bury all of those acorns and then they won't remember where they put them. Next summer, I'll have little oak trees springing up all over.

There were several bird feeders around the yard, and throughout the day he saw cardinals, blue jays and various other types of birds. Squirrels were continually climbing into the bird feeders and that would bring the blue jays on, squawking at the squirrels and sometimes even simulating a dive-bomber and diving in at them.

Jay's thoughts turned towards the mountains. He'd loved hiking in the mountains in his younger years, but hadn't been in a long while. One of the reasons he'd decided to live here in the Valley was due to the proximity to the Blue Ridge Mountains. He thought that soon, he needed to head back up and do some hiking.

The afternoon progressed with Jay drinking beer and watching the animals. A few hours later, he heard Angela pull into the driveway. He heard the front door open. She called for him, but he didn't answer. A moment later, she appeared at the back door.

"What are you doing out here?" she asked.

"I'm just watching the critters run around the yard." He stood up to give her a hug and stumbled a little bit as he stepped towards her.

"Jay, you're drunk. Why are you doing this? Think about the kids and me. Don't do this to yourself." She walked closer to him, but he really didn't respond.

He took another swig. Angela grimaced and then walked into the house. He sat out there until the sun was starting to set. The great thing about having so much space around him was when he wanted to take a leak, he could just get up and do so off the edge of the deck. None of the neighbors could see him and to a guy, this was one of the better pleasures in life.

Angela, on the other hand, had never understood this and now she couldn't understand his drinking. She walked back out as the sky was darkening and asked him if he was going to come in for dinner.

"What did ya cook?" he asked, slurring his words ever so slightly.

"Your favorite. Grilled salmon, broccoli and wild brown rice."

"I'll be right there."

"Make sure you wash up. I saw you taking a piss off the back deck. I just hope none of the neighbors saw you doing that. What would they think?"

"No one saw me and so what if they did. This is my house and I can do what I want to." Jay's voice rose as he said this. He was prepared to say more, but he stayed silent. Angela did as well.

They ate in dead silence for a few minutes. The kids were still at Angela's mother's house. Jay thought briefly about them. Marie was in third grade and Tim was in eighth grade at the middle school, which was located right next to the elementary school. Both kids had always done well in school and both parents had always been extremely proud of them.

Angela eventually asked if he liked the food.

"It's pretty good," Jay mumbled. He was still just half picking at his food and not eating much of it.

After dinner, Jay made his way into the TV room, where he sat drinking his final three beers of the twelve-pack. Damn, I haven't drunk this much in years, he thought.

Angela came out once and tried to talk to him, but gave up after he started cursing at her.

By 11PM, Jay was sleeping and could not be awakened. Angela pulled his shoes off of him, put a pillow under his head, went and got a blanket and covered him up.

Jay slept on the couch, dreaming of Moe. Moe was coming at him and Jay kept firing and firing with no effect. He was tossing and turning and even grunted as if in pain two or three times. His dreams continued, sometimes causing him to wake up, covered in sweat and shaking. Moe was starting to haunt him.

Sometime in the wee hours of the morning when the sky was blackest, Jay drifted off into a deep, dreamless sleep.

CHAPTER 5

Angela woke up at 6AM as she normally did. After rinsing her face quickly in the bathroom sink, she walked out to check on Jay. He was still sleeping soundly on the living room couch. She watched him for a minute or two, seeing his muscular chest rise and fall with each breath. She heard a slight snore on every third breath or so.

What is happening with him? she thought. He's always told me he wouldn't hesitate to shoot someone if he thought they were trying to kill him. Now, it's really wearing on him. It's only been a few days, but he's drinking too much and he's cursing me like he's never done before.

She was glad that her mother was going to keep the kids for the rest of the week. Her mother lived just down the street from the schools and Tim and

Marie liked it when they stayed there because they could walk to school instead of riding the bus.

Angela hoped Jay would snap out of his "funk" soon and hopefully everything could just return to normal.

She decided against waking him up. She turned around and walked to the bathroom to take a shower. Looking into the mirror, she could see the beginning of small lines around the corner of her eyes. She was still a beautiful woman, but she could see that the years were starting to take their toll. Her hair was still a pretty golden color, but some gray was starting to creep in. Sometimes, she wished that she could return to the life she'd had when she was a young eighteen-year-old fresh out of high school. That was before she'd ever met Jay.

She met Jay during her senior year of college. He had a class with her and they'd worked together on a science project. It didn't take long before they were dating. Within a few months Jay asked her to marry him.

Looking back into the mirror, she noticed she still had a firm, shapely body. She did have to work harder now to keep it looking as good as it did, but she noticed she still turned guy's heads when she walked by. She smiled slightly at this thought.

After showering, Angela went to the kitchen and made herself a waffle. She placed some blueberries on top of it. She had a cup of black coffee as well. It was almost time for her to leave. She walked back out to check on Jay.

"Jay," she said softly. He did not stir. He's tired,

she thought, so I'll let him sleep. He needs his rest.

Angela wrote a short note saying she hoped he'd slept well and there were waffles in the freezer and blueberries in the refrigerator. She also said for Jay to call her when he woke up. Her last sentence was "I love you."

It was pushing 10 o'clock when Jay started stirring. Damn, I feel rough, he thought. His head was pounding. His tongue was swollen and felt like it had been rubbed with a piece of sandpaper.

After taking a leak and washing his face, he went to the kitchen to make a cup of coffee. He saw the note from Angela and figured he would wait a bit to call her. She wouldn't know what time he had awakened, so there was really no need to call her right away.

Moe. Damn. Why is his name popping back into my mind? Jay had just stepped out of the shower. He looked into the slightly cloudy bathroom mirror. He still had bags under his bloodshot eyes. He hadn't shaved and he noticed a touch of gray in his beard. He normally shaved every day. He now had several days of growth on his face.

However, after wiping off the mirror and stepping back, he noticed he still had a muscular build. He worked out with weights quite regularly and it still showed.

After showering, Jay went out and ate a bowl of oatmeal for breakfast. He wasn't in the mood for waffles. He also called Angela and talked to her for a few minutes, assuring her that he was okay.

After hanging up the phone, Jay walked outside

and picked up the newspaper. There it was, right on the front page. **"State Police Clear Police Officer."**

They'd printed another picture of Jay that had been taken a few years back at an awards ceremony. I bet Eli gave that picture to the media, Jay thought. Jay knew how Eli worked. By supplying the media with a picture of him receiving an award for meritorious service, it would just help to create a more positive image.

Jay sighed deeply and sat down in his blue La-Z-Boy recliner. He read through the article, but it was the same stuff from the past few days, just rehashed. It did highlight the fact that he was cleared of any wrongdoing and the Chief was quoted as saying Jay would be back to work in a few days.

Sure, Chief, I'll be back to work in a few days. Why not, nothing has changed at all, Jay thought sarcastically.

This time at the store, Jay picked up two cases of Icehouse beer.

By the time Angela returned home from work, Jay was on his way to being drunk again. Angela told him he was drinking too much and he needed to stop.

"Hair of the Dog, babe, Hair of the Dog," Jay shouted at her.

"What the hell are you talking about?" Angela screamed back at him.

Jay loudly explained when a person was hung over, the best cure was to take another drink and that was called hair of the dog. Jay wasn't quite sure if the definition he gave Angela was correct, but he reasoned his non-drinking wife wouldn't know if he was right or wrong.

Jay walked out to the deck again, even though it was quite chilly. He sat there for several hours, watching the sunset. He'd stopped counting his drinks, but he thought he'd probably had at least twelve, if not more. At least it was only beer, and not real liquor, he thought.

Jay had just finished off another twelve-ounce bottle of Icehouse, when he decided he would take a leak and then head in to bed.

He walked to the edge of the deck and started taking a whiz. He finished and was zipping up his trousers when he must have taken a step forward. The next thing he knew, he was hitting the ground. The deck was only three feet high, but it sure hurt when he fell and wasn't expecting it. He rubbed his knee where it had hit something hard.

Jay sat up and wiped some blood from his nose. Nothing seemed to be broken, at least not that he could tell tonight. What's happening to me? That damned Moe Jackson. He just had to start shooting at me.

He decided to drink just one more beer and then call it a night. That final one tasted as good as his first one, if not better, but he still kept thinking about Moe.

Knowing that Angela was a light sleeper and knowing he was stumbling a little bit, Jay decided just to sleep on the couch. Why not, he thought. If I wake up Angela, she'll just get pissed off at me.

Mark Kearney

He lay on the couch, but could not get to sleep. He wondered what Moe felt like when he took his final breath. He thought about how he felt, when he first realized he had killed Moe Jackson. Something about all of this made him smile.

CHAPTER 6

Jay saw Doctor Miller exactly three weeks to the day after shooting Moe. Prior to seeing the psychologist, Jay had plenty of time to do a lot of thinking. He'd been having a fairly rough time in the weeks following the shooting of Moe. Everyone was telling him the shooting was justified. He knew it was justified. Any good cop would have done the exact same thing, damn it.

At first, he theorized, he'd fallen into a state of depression in the days following Moe's death. He started drinking more than ever and that just compounded the problem. Shit, though, he was still drinking way too much, but he didn't think he was depressed any longer.

The more he thought about Moe's death, the more he felt he'd done the right thing. Moe was one of the scum that the earth needed to be rid of. He wanted his kids to grow up in a good world, and with toads like Moe and the thousands of others out there, what chance did good kids have of making a success of themselves?

Now, there was one less. Jay wondered if he would ever be in another situation where he would be justified to use deadly force. As the days passed on in those first three weeks, Jay thought of different scenarios where he would be authorized to use deadly force. The only thing though, is he had been the first police officer in over fifteen years to use deadly force in this town. If he killed a suspect again, they would take a harder look at him.

What if I killed someone, but no one knew it was me that did it?

He didn't mention these thoughts to the doctor when he saw him. As Jay stepped into his office, he quickly scanned the room as all good cops do upon entering a room. The typical couch that was always mentioned when dealing with a psychologist's office was missing. Instead, there were three, black, comfortable looking chairs. There were some framed certificates on the walls as well as some beautiful outdoor photographs.

As Jay entered the room, Doctor Miller stood up. To say the doctor was large was an understatement. He must have been no more than six feet tall, but he was probably over 300 pounds. He had gray hair and a short gray beard.

"Jay, how are you, son? It's been awhile since I've talked with you. I'm sorry it has to be under these circumstances." Doc and Jay had first met five years ago at a PD picnic. They'd hit it off almost immediately. Jay had been surprised when he found out that Joe Miller was the psychologist for the PD.

"I'm doing okay, Doc. It was rough for the first week or so after I shot Moe, but I'm feeling better with each passing day."

"Tell me a little bit about the past few weeks."

"I made this appointment a few days after I shot Moe and I was quite depressed at the time, but I think I'm doing much better now," Jay related to Doc.

Doc asked him several different questions to get Jay talking. Jay always felt very relaxed around Doc Miller and he found himself talking a lot about his wife and kids. The one thing Jay did not even hint at with the Doc was his thoughts of killing someone else.

Jay spent about an hour altogether talking with Doc. At the end of the session, Doc shook hands with Jay and pronounced his mind as fit as a fiddle.

"Call me anytime you want to talk, but I don't think you need to see me professionally again."

"Thanks, Doc. I'll be seeing you around."

Jay walked out of the office feeling pretty good. It always cheered him up when he talked with the doctor. But somewhere in the back of his mind, he had a feeling of darkness that was penetrating his brain. The thought of killing someone made him smile all the more. He thought something had to be wrong if he felt this way, but Doc had just cleared him, so he must be okay.

After he got into his truck, he sat for several minutes with his eyes closed. Once again, a mental image appeared of Moe Jackson coming after him. He had that wild look in his eyes and he kept saying over and over that he wanted to kill Jay.

Jay quickly banished that thought from his mind. However, he still saw blood and death. It wasn't Moe, though. It was someone else dead at Jay's feet.

Smiling, Jay opened his eyes and shook his head to clear his thoughts. Why did he keep thinking about killing someone? He knew why, but it scared him that he was having these thoughts. Damn that Moe Jackson. If it wasn't for him, none of this would have happened and he wouldn't be thinking these crazy things.

That evening, while watching TV and sipping on his fifth beer of the night, he started thinking about how he could kill another person. There were so many ways to do this. He had seen many of those ways during his tenure of being a police officer. He thought of the various homicides he had either worked or assisted in working. He thought of the ones where the killer had been caught and the several where no suspect had ever been identified.

He thought about his two children again. They were in bed sleeping, but sometimes he wondered about ever bringing them into this world. The world is a screwed-up place. Did he make a mistake to have them?

Angela walked into the room at about ten o'clock and said she would be going to bed soon. Jay just nodded his head and didn't say anything. Angela stood there for a few seconds and then sat down next to him on the couch.

"Honey, you know I love you very much, but your drinking is concerning me. You've been drinking every day and not just a beer or two, but a six-pack at a time."

"Angela, you haven't been through what I have and if I want to drink a few fucking beers, I will do just that."

"Come on, Jay. Why do you keep cursing me? You never did that before, but now you seem to always be saying F this and F that. Please, Jay, don't do this to me and the kids."

Jay got up from the couch, walked into the kitchen and pulled another beer out of the refrigerator. He walked back into the living room and sat down in his recliner. Angela was just sitting there staring at him with tears in her eyes.

Jay took a quick drink and then belched loudly. He smiled at Angela when this happened, but she didn't smile back. He took another sip as Angela stood up from the couch.

"I'm going to bed, Jay. How long are you going to stay out here and drink?"

"As long as I want and I'm going to drink as many beers as I want."

As he said that he turned the bottle back and started chugging his beer like a college kid at a party.

As he put the bottle down and wiped his mouth, Angela just said, "Thanks, Jay," as she turned and walked back to the bedroom.

Jay sat out there for several more hours, just drinking one beer after another. He kept thinking about killing another toad and how this would help out the world. Wasn't the world a better place without Moe Jackson around?

Jay kept running different scenarios through his mind. How could he kill another person and get away with it? He thought of a lot of different things, but he kept coming to the same conclusion that it would not work or that he wouldn't get away with it.

Once again, a sense of dread started coming into Jay's mind. This feeling of darkness scared him. When it occurred, it engulfed his mind and all he could think about was killing someone. He knew that it was because of Moe's death. He was finishing up his thirteenth beer of the night when it hit him that if he *did* kill someone else, it would probably cause the feeling of dread to diminish.

CHAPTER 7

Jay was working daylight. He and Sean O'Hara were working on Calvert Street doing some "community policing." Community policing, yeah right, thought Jay. They were trying to clean up the drug addicts and the homeless in the area.

Sean was the son of the Irish Deputy Chief, Tom O'Hara. Jay was getting tired of Sean. He had worked with him in the past and what he didn't like was that Sean was ramrod straight. On a day like today, dealing with the scum of Cutler, they needed to bend the rules ever so slightly.

If he were with anyone else, they would have. However, since Sean was the son of the second in command, Jay felt it best to hold his tongue with him.

They came to an empty three-story building. Jay

turned the handle on the door and the door opened. A stench of stale urine and beer came pouring out the door.

He heard the scurrying of feet inside and some muffled voices.

Jay pulled out his flashlight and his .40 caliber Glock pistol. He entered the building and shined his flashlight around. He caught two older guys in the beam of his light and got a glimpse of someone else running up the stairs.

"Sean, stay here with these two. I'm going up the stairs to get the others."

"Are you sure you should go up there alone? I'm going to call for back up. Wait for someone else to get here."

"If I wait, they may get to the roof and jump over to another building and get away. I'm going up."

"Ok, I'm going to check these two and if they aren't wanted, I'm going to cut them loose and I'll be up in just a sec."

"All right."

Jay slowly climbed the stairs to the second floor. This floor was unlike the first floor. The first floor was basically one big open area. The second floor had walls and it appeared this used to be where some offices were. There was one long hallway, with rooms on one side.

"Damn, I really should wait on some back up, but I'm going to find these fuckers," Jay whispered to himself.

Jay still had his Glock in his right hand and his flashlight in his left. He slowly walked the hallway until he came to the first office. Peering in the room, he could tell it was empty.

He continued on, finding the next two rooms empty as well. But, as he was approaching the fourth and final room, Jay heard the scuffling of feet inside the room.

Jay stopped and thought for a minute. Sean was downstairs if he needed him. But if someone in the room had a gun, they would have the advantage on Jay.

Jay, after hesitating for just a minute, kicked the door open and jumped in, flashlight shining around the room, Glock pointed and his voice shouting, "On the ground, on the ground!"

There were two scruffy, middle-aged guys in the room. Both got onto the floor, holding their hands out from their bodies. They had been through this before, Jay could tell.

Jay went over and patted each one down. Finding nothing on them, he told them to get up and walk downstairs. They did, Jay still holding his Glock on them, just in case.

When they got downstairs, the other two guys were being told to move on by Sean. Sean looked surprised to see Jay bringing the two downstairs at gunpoint.

"What happened? Are they giving you trouble?"

"I haven't ID'd them yet. I patted them down quickly, but not that thoroughly."

Sean talked to the two apparently homeless gentlemen. After getting ID cards from them, he ran some 10-29 checks on them that came back negative. 10-29 checks are wanted checks. Sean cut them loose.

After they walked out, Sean turned to Jay. "Why didn't you wait for back up to get here? That was risky going up there alone, not knowing who was up there."

"Hey, not a problem, man. It all turned out well. I figured they were just some of the local homeless guys. It all turned out cool."

Sean didn't seem to like this too much, but he didn't say anything else. They did go back up to the third floor to check that no one else was in the building. It was empty.

Leaving the building and coming back out into the sunlight, Jay squinted. After being inside a dark building using a flashlight, it sure seemed bright outside.

Jay and Sean continued walking Calvert Street for another hour. They found a few more homeless guys, but they never did find any drugs or make any arrests. But, they cleared everyone out and told them that if they were found here again, they would be charged with trespassing.

They did their best to secure the doors that they could. Most could be closed and locked. But, the lock was busted on the three-story building they had searched earlier, so they could only pull the door shut tight.

"I'll contact the property owner and tell him he needs to secure the building better," Jay told Sean.

"Okay. Let's get out of here," Sean replied.

Getting into their respective police cruisers, they

told each other they'd meet up later.

This would be a great spot to kill someone, Jay thought. Every building on this block and several other adjacent blocks were empty. Now that they had cleared them out, they might stay empty for a while.

* * *

Ah, maybe one day, maybe one day. Jay drove off, thinking again of Moe and the possibility of killing someone else.

CHAPTER 8

It was the middle of December. The seasons were ready to change from autumn to winter. The weather had gone from being brisk and chilly to snow flurries. The high temperature of the day was 33 degrees. Christmas was right around the corner.

Driving around, Jay saw many people had their Christmas lights up and Christmas trees could be seen through many windows around town. The city had placed Christmas wreaths on many light poles and there was an air of holiday spirit. The sign at the mall said that Santa Claus would be there each night from 5PM to 9PM.

Jay was on routine patrol. He'd been back to work for about five weeks. His life was just rolling along, but where he would end up, he didn't know. He really didn't think much about Moe anymore.

However, he was drinking a lot. Angela still pleaded with him to stop, but she was starting to slow down a bit. It was common for him to put away a six-pack a day after working a 12-hour shift. He would also drink a large portion of a case of beer on his days off.

Jay noticed the kids were acting differently toward him as well, but he really didn't think too much about that. He was their father and they had better respect him or he would show them who was boss.

It was one o'clock in the morning. Jay had been driving around for the past two hours without a single call or traffic stop. It was fairly unusual on a night shift for it to be so quiet, but that was the life of a cop.

You could be busy as a bee one day, going from car accident to a domestic to a robbery within a few hours. Or, you could go an entire shift with only one or two calls of a minor nature.

Jay turned on Calvert Street and cruised along slowly. This street was in a rough section of town and it was very dark here. There were a lot of empty, run-down buildings that vagrants would hang out in from time to time. It seemed fairly quiet though, as most people were probably indoors due to the cold. Of course, he and Sean O' Hara had just come through here on their last daylight shift, three days ago, and chased all the homeless out. So, the place might still be empty.

At that moment, Jay spotted someone walking. The person turned to look at Jay's car. It appeared to be a female in her mid 20's who seemed to be crying. Jay decided to pull over to check on her. Normally, he would have radioed in that he would be off with a white female on Calvert Street, but this time he didn't.

Jay called the girl over to his car and asked her what was wrong. She was dressed in fairly nice clothes and she looked out of place in this neighborhood. She told him that she'd been fighting with her boyfriend; she had gotten out of his car a few blocks back and started walking. Jay asked her if she was cold because she only had a thin jacket on. She nodded that she was.

The girl appeared a bit nervous or scared. A lot of people were when they were not used to talking to the police. She was trembling slightly and her lip quivered. However, after a few minutes of talking with him, she began to calm down. Jay asked her if she wanted a ride and she hesitated to answer. She started to open her mouth to answer, but then shut it. Jay shut off his cruiser and stepped out.

He shivered upon getting out and stepping into the cool air. He was wearing his short-sleeve uniform shirt and his jacket was lying in the passenger seat of his car. She stepped back momentarily, but then she laughed and said something about him being a cop and taking care of her. Jay was attracted to her. She was cute, blond, young and seemed to have a nice body. She was wearing a pair of dark slacks and a light colored sweater. Yeah, she was cute, but by the way she was acting, she seemed to be a rich, spoiled brat who was used to having things her own way.

They started talking and she and Jay sat down on the curb, next to the same empty three-story building that he and Sean had cleared out a few days ago. She told him about her fight with her boyfriend. Jay really wasn't listening to her. Once again, he saw an image of Moe coming after him. He watched the girl's Adam's apple bobbing up and down as she spoke.

He glanced around. The streets were deserted, as were the sidewalks. He did not see a single car or person.

Suddenly, without warning, Jay pulled his Spyder-Co knife from his pocket and held it against her throat. The girl's blue eyes opened wide in terror and her red mouth formed an O. She started trembling all over.

"Get up," he ordered.

He checked the door of the old empty building and it was still unlocked. He opened the door and pushed her inside. It was eerie and pitch black until he pulled out his flashlight and turned it on. As the light flickered on the walls, he told her to walk up the stairs to the second floor.

Getting to the second floor, the room was just like Jay remembered it. The hallway was in front of them and there were old offices going down one side. Pigeon droppings were all over the hallway. He saw a few beer cans and bottles littered about.

"What are you going to do to me?" she whispered in a shaky voice.

"Be quiet." Jay stood there for what seemed to

be several minutes, but was actually only seconds. His knife was in his hand and his gun was in its holster.

The girl started crying softly at first. She begged Jay not to hurt her, getting more hysterical second by second. Then, she bolted, running down the hallway. Jay didn't chase her immediately. He knew she couldn't get out from that end of the room.

Jay kept thinking about Moe coming after him and how his eyes had been gleaming and how he had kept pointing his gun at Jay. He followed after the girl, finding her in the last, dark room. He shined his light on her. Her mouth opened in a scream. He couldn't hear her, but he knew she was screaming.

Her neck was smooth and inviting. The veins in it were pulsating. Her heart must have been beating rapidly, as her breaths were coming in quick succession. Jay walked closer to her. She was trapped and looked like a caged tiger. Jay knew he had to act quickly.

He felt his hand holding the knife start to move. He saw it all happening in slow motion. His arm reached out, pulled back, and then swung forward with the knife; slicing the girl from one ear to the other. Blood gushed from her throat. She grabbed her throat with one hand and reached for him with the other, missing. She fell to the ground. She was trying to scream, but it was just coming out as a gurgling sound.

Blood was running out of her throat. It pulsated out, in time with the beating of her heart. She was still alive, so Jay stabbed her in the chest... then again and again.

Jay stood back and looked at the still body of the once attractive girl. A puddle of blood had formed all around her. He looked at his hands and saw blood all over them. He was wearing short sleeves and blood had splashed onto his forearms.

What have I done? thought Jay. Think, think, think.

Ok, if no one has seen us, what evidence have I left behind? Did I touch anything? Jay took a handkerchief out of his back pocket. He went to the door and wiped off the handle. I'd better do more than that, he thought. He went back to his cruiser and got some alcohol-based hand cleaner. He sprayed that on the door handle and wiped it off.

What else? No footprints as he had been on the street, the sidewalk and then inside a building. Jay couldn't think of any clues he left behind, as long as no one had seen him there. He still had to get away and get cleaned up before he was in the clear.

Jay knew about a public bathroom that was in the next block over. It was locked up at night, but he had a key to it. The cops all knew what bathrooms they could use. Police officers could never take for granted that they would have a proper opportunity to eat or drink, or even take a leak. He never knew if the next call to come across the radio might tie him up for hours.

Jay made it to the bathroom without seeing another person or car. He washed up. He went to his cruiser and wiped down his seat and his steering wheel to make sure there was no blood stains on it.

As he drove away from the area, Jay felt pretty good. He had just killed another person. As far as he could tell, he'd gotten completely away with it. Plus, there was a good chance that no one would find the body for several days. With it being cold, it wouldn't start stinking up the neighborhood for even longer.

* * *

Jay was surprised when just two days later there was a story in the news about the discovery of a murdered girl's body in an old, deserted office building on Calvert Street.

It seems the boyfriend had tried to contact the girl the next day to apologize and found out she'd never made it home. He'd waited a day, thinking she would appear, but when she didn't, he called the police and told them what had happened. The police had searched the area where the boyfriend had last seen the girl. They had been the ones to find the body.

Jay had been off for the past two days. When he came back, he was on day work. He ran into Dave in the hallway and asked him what had happened with the murdered girl.

"I don't know, man. There were no signs of a sexual assault. But, it looked like someone was really pissed at her."

"So how'd it happen?"

"There were no signs of a struggle. Her throat was sliced from ear to ear. She was also stabbed thirteen times in her chest."

"Did anyone see anything?"

"There are no witnesses that have come forward and there is no motive as far as I can find."

"What about the boyfriend?" Jay asked.

"His alibi checks out. He said after the girl got out of his car, he drove home to his parents' house."

"Do you have his car? Did you find anything in it?"

"We seized his car and got a search warrant for his house, but we didn't turn up a single piece of evidence implicating him in her death. Plus, he is quite distraught. I've talked to a lot of people that knew both of them and everyone speaks very highly of him. If he did it, he covered his tracks well and he is very upset about all of this. I don't think he did it, but I don't know who did."

"Well, good luck buddy. I hope you can get this one solved," Jay said as he slapped Dave on the back.

Jay walked outside to his cruiser and started it up. *Yep, I'm a cop and I'm here to protect and serve,* he thought as he looked into the rearview mirror.

CHAPTER 9

Several days later, Jay was working his twelve-hour shift. He had had only a few calls all day. He thought quite a bit about the killing of the girl, but surprisingly, he did not think very much about Moe. He'd read in the paper that the girl's name was Allison Berry and she was an only child of wealthy parents.

It struck Jay as kind of funny that the one person he decided to kill was not a local toad. Looking into his rearview mirror, Jay wondered what was happening to him. He did not feel any sadness or remorse about the unnecessary death of the girl. He actually felt a little bit excited about it.

Late in the afternoon, he walked into the PD as Dave walked out. Jay stopped to talk with him for a few minutes. He told Jay he was frustrated by the lack of clues in the homicide.

"There is absolutely no motive for anyone to have killed the girl, so I'm thinking it was just a random thing, perhaps done by someone just passing through," Dave said.

"We've been having more and more homeless people coming into town here of late. It could have been somebody like that who killed her."

"Yeah, but if it was someone passing through who did her in, he could be anywhere by now. If he hopped on the interstate, who knows where he is."

"If no witnesses turn up, the chances of me solving this case may be pretty slim. I hope not, but I really have nothing to go on."

"Dave, you're good. You'll figure it out, buddy."

"The autopsy didn't even turn anything up. The girl was not sexually molested. It did turn up a hair and fibers on her body, but odds are most of that came from her lying on the floor in the room where she was killed. Over the past few years, we've had numerous homeless folks and drug addicts found in those rooms."

Jay wished Dave luck with the case and told him if there was anything he could do to help him, just to let him know.

Jay walked into the PD. He went to the break room to get a snack from one of the machines. On the bulletin board, he saw a poster made up with the dead girl's picture on it, along with a request that if anyone knew anything about this case to call the police or to stay anonymous and to call Crime Stoppers.

Crime Stoppers was a program where if someone knew information about a criminal case, a wanted person, or some other police matter, they could call and stay completely anonymous while providing the information. If the information led to an arrest or to the solving of a case, the caller could be eligible for a cash reward of up to $1000.

The PD had been having a lot of success with the Crime Stoppers program. It seems for a little bit of money, people would turn their own family members in. Jay hoped again that he had not been seen that night.

The only slip-up that he could think of was the fact that he had been in a marked cruiser, and he had parked on Calvert Street for fifteen or twenty minutes. If anyone called Crime Stoppers and said they had seen his cruiser, that could easily point to him being a suspect. If this happened and they checked his car out they could probably find some clues in there. He had cleaned it the best he could that night, but under the scrutiny of a detective bent on finding an innocent girl's killer, some small smattering of blood could turn up.

The good thing was Dave had just told him there were no leads, so maybe no one had seen him and he was completely in the clear. He smiled once again because he really thought he had committed the perfect crime. It may have not been quite perfect, but he was going to get away with it.

The next time, there would be no mistakes.

Jay's twelve-hour shift came to an end at 7PM. Upon getting home, he walked in the house and grabbed a beer from the fridge before even taking his uniform off. Angela looked at him, but she didn't say anything.

* * *

Jay was back into work bright and early at 7AM the next morning, even though he was up until a little past midnight drinking a total of six or seven beers.

As Jay drove around town, he thought about Cutler. Cutler was not a very big town. It had a population of about 75,000 people. It was big enough that normally there was a fair amount of excitement at work, but small enough that the town didn't have the crime a big city does.

Cutler was only two hours away from the City of Richmond, a direct shot on the interstate. This would bring in some of the riff raff from the larger city from time to time. No doubt many of them thought Cutler was just a small country town where the police didn't know how to do their work.

During the afternoon, Jay ventured over to Calvert Street for the first time since the night when he'd killed the girl. It still amazed him that he'd actually gone through with killing her and had gotten away with it. And the funny thing was, this seemed to have slowed down the appearance of Moe in his dreams.

Now he was thinking about the next time. He thought he should go to Richmond. Cutler was just too small and if he killed another person in this town, it would just increase the chances that he would get caught.

However, in Richmond, a homicide would just be one of hundreds that happened every year. He wasn't positive, but he thought the rate of solving homicides in Richmond was a little less than fifty percent. And this was even when the majority of the homicides were just drug murders by other druggies slaughtering each other.

Jay smiled. He was a cop and he knew how to do things. He wouldn't make the same mistakes he did the first time. But since he had made mistakes and still got away with it, he knew if he killed someone in Richmond he would get away with it for certain.

* * *

Two weeks later, Jay was working night shift again. He was patrolling through one of the many parks in town. Christmas had been three days prior. Some of the evergreen trees in the park were still decorated with Christmas lights. The color on the trees added to the beauty in the park.

While riding through Forest View Park, he saw a young person walking down one of the trails. Jay yelled over to him. The kid stopped and turned. It was Tony White. Tony was one of those punk boys. Even though he was only fourteen, most of the police officers knew who he was. He was always getting into some kind of trouble.

Surprisingly, Tony didn't take off running when

Jay called him. Instead, he turned and walked toward him. Jay got out of his cruiser and looked around. The park was dark and deserted. It was almost 3AM. The parked closed at dusk. They normally didn't have much of a problem with people coming into the park after hours. Not after the new curfew ordinance which limited teens under seventeen to being off the street by midnight.

Tony was a fairly small light skinned black male, about 5'4", and he would have been lucky to weigh one hundred pounds soaking wet. Tony's mother had been and probably still was a crack addict. His father had been locked up in prison for the past eight years.

Tony approached Jay. Jay gave another quick look around and stepped up to meet Tony where they would be in the shadows. Tony stopped about three feet away and asked, "What's up, man? I ain't done nothin'."

Jay began to tell him there was no trespassing after dark in the park. He got a strange feeling at that moment. He saw an image of Tony lying face down on the ground. Without any warning, Jay drew back his fist. He punched Tony as hard as he could in the throat.

Tony dropped to the ground almost instantly. He was gasping for air. It appeared he was unconscious. His breaths were ragged and gurgling. A bit of blood was coming out of the corner of his mouth.

It was dark. Jay could see the Christmas lights on the trees, but they were on the other side of the park. He and Tony were in the shadows. Looking around, he didn't see anyone at all. He bent over and listened to Tony struggling for breath. Jay rolled him completely onto his back and stood over him.

Then, with Tony lying on his back, breathing short, raspy-sounding breaths, Jay placed his boot on Tony's throat and pressed down as hard as he could. Tony's body jerked sporadically several times. Jay just pressed down harder. He must have stayed in that position for two full minutes. He waited until all movement had stopped.

He waited another minute just to be sure, and then removed his boot from Tony's throat. Jay bent over to check for a pulse and did not feel one.

Jay picked up the limp body and threw it over his shoulder. He walked to his car, opened up his trunk and placed Tony's body in there with all of the miscellaneous police crap. Traffic cones, a fingerprint kit, a fire extinguisher, yellow police tape, a yardstick, biohazard bags and a box of road flares. It was a tight fit, but Jay was able to get the trunk shut.

Jay pulled out of the park, glancing at the clock, which now read 3:12. Tony's mother probably had no idea where her son was. As far as Jay knew, Tony had not stayed regularly at his mother's house for several years now. His attendance in school was very poor. Sometimes he would miss a week straight before he would show back up.

Seeing that it was a Saturday night, Tony's mother was probably passed out somewhere herself. She probably wouldn't expect to see Tony at all on Sunday.

About three blocks from the park, Jay passed another marked cruiser. Keith was driving it and as they passed, Keith called him on the radio. Using police jargon, he asked him to meet him in the park.

Jay answered in the affirmative. He swung his cruiser around, trying not to think about Tony's body in his trunk.

CHAPTER 10

Jay felt remarkably relaxed as he pulled his cruiser alongside Keith's cruiser, which he had parked about fifty yards from where Jay had just pulled out with the body in his trunk. As Jay rolled down his window, Keith said something to him about it being a boring night.

"It sure is. We haven't had a call in hours. I haven't even heard any cop make a traffic stop," Jay answered.

Keith was close to Jay's age, in his mid to late thirties. His hair was blond, but currently he had a short buzz cut. His neck bulged from his shirt collar. Keith was not that tall, 5'9" or so, but he was built like a brick house. He started telling Jay about his boys and how they were doing on the local high school basketball team. The boys played baseball in the spring, football in the fall, basketball in the winter and they both swam on an aquatics team that was in the pool almost year around.

While Keith was talking, Jay was thinking about Tony's body. He had to get it out of there quick.

There was a reservoir just on the outskirts of town that was completely full due to the wet year they'd been having. A plan began to form deep in the recesses of his brain.

Yawning and telling Keith that he was falling asleep just sitting there, Jay said he had to get out and start driving around. It was the hour of the night when officers would drift back into their assigned districts to do their business checks.

Once Jay drove out of the park, he headed back in the direction of the PD. He didn't see anyone standing outside so he pulled up next to his truck and took out a short coil of rope that he always kept behind the seat. He quickly cut off a section about eight feet long, sticking that piece into his cruiser and returning the rest to the area behind his seat.

Jay proceeded out of the parking lot and headed in the direction of the reservoir. He remembered seeing some concrete blocks lying on an old construction site that was right along the way to the reservoir. Driving up to the site, he didn't see a single car or person about. He pulled over, hopped out and grabbed two of the cinderblocks. He placed them in the back seat of his cruiser.

From there, he continued out of town on Route 16. He drove to a remote area around the reservoir he knew from his fishing days. He pulled in and shut off his lights, parking his car as close as he could to the edge of the bank.

Jay had often been swimming here as a child. He knew that in this spot, with the water as high as it was, it at least twenty-five or thirty feet straight down. A teenager had drowned in that very spot when Jay was younger and they had outlawed swimming after that. Fishermen still came, but not really many of them.

Jay got both the cinderblocks and the rope out of his car. He cut it into two, four-foot long sections. Looking around again to make sure that no one else was nearby, Jay opened the trunk.

Tony was lying there amidst the miscellaneous police crap. His body was folded over in what would have been a painful position had he still been alive. His chest was pressing against his knees. Jay lifted the limp body out of the trunk. Rigor mortis was already starting to set in. There was a trickle of blood that had run out of his mouth. The stench of urine was strong, as Tony's bladder had emptied itself after Jay had punched him.

Jay placed the stiffening body on the loose gravel about two feet from the drop-off. He took each section of rope and tied one end to each foot and the other end to each block. Jay wasn't sure how long the rope would last in the water, but he figured it would last long enough that Tony's body would probably be almost completely decomposed or eaten by the fish or the eels that inhabited this body of water by the time the ropes broke free.

Jay checked Tony's pockets to make sure that

nothing was in them that could float out and identify him. He found some loose change and an empty pack of cigarettes and a lighter. He left it all in Tony's pockets.

Just as Jay was ready to pick Tony up, he heard a twig snap. He turned, pulling his Glock out of its holster. He didn't see anything and turned back to his business.

As he prepared to lift Tony again, the hair on the back of his neck stiffened and he felt eyes boring into him. As he turned again, he saw a dog.

The dog approached, growling, baring its teeth. Its ears are laid back, and it looked as if it is prepared to lunge.

Jay yanked his asp out of its holder and snapped it open. The dog heard it and looked at Jay, still growling. He raised the asp up as if he was going to strike the dog. That was all it took. The dog, seeing Jay raise his arm and hearing Jay's yell, slowly backed away, then turned and ran off into the trees.

A previous owner must have beaten him before, thought Jay. He glanced at his watch. The digital display read 4:17. Just a few more hours until daylight would be here. This time of the year had some of the shortest days of the year. The sun wouldn't rise until almost 7AM.

He bent over and dragged Tony to the edge, then rolled him over and pushed the cinderblocks behind him. He heard a splash and then no more.

Glancing around again, he still didn't see anybody and he saw no signs of the dog. He shined his Mag-

Lite quickly over the water. Besides seeing a small air bubble, there was no sign of Tony.

This went better than I expected, thought Jay. He went back to his cruiser and popped open the trunk once more. Shining his light into the trunk, he looked around to make sure there were no obvious signs of Tony having been in the trunk. He didn't notice anything. The trunks of the cruisers were normally a mess, so he moved around some of the items to cover up the area where Tony's body had been.

His PD was still one of the few in the state that did not allow the officers to have take-home cars. This meant when his shift was over, someone from the next shift would be getting into his car.

The bad thing about that was he was constantly finding a mess that another officer would leave in the car. The good thing was, with four different shifts and four different officers driving the cruiser, within a few days any minute evidence that he may have in his car would more than likely be destroyed.

He remembered at the start of his shift that the off-going officer had told him he had picked up a sick cat that had maggots coming out of its stomach. The officer had to stick the cat in the trunk so he could take him to a remote spot where he could dispose of the cat properly.

Thinking about all of this made Jay feel a lot better about everything. Odds are, no one would notice Tony was missing for several days. It would probably be at least a week until his mother even bothered to report him missing. With Tony's history, people would just think that he had run off and that he'd turn back up eventually.

Jay snickered out loud. He got into his cruiser, started it up and turned it around. Before pulling out of the parking area, he gave one more look around.

Once again, he had gotten away with committing a murder. He was good, and with this one, he was confident that no one would even know that Tony was dead for many, many months or maybe even never. And that meant, as long as Jay kept his mouth shut about what he had done, no one would ever know a thing.

Getting back onto Route 16, Jay drove to town, not passing another car all the way back into his assigned district. He drove around for several more hours without a single call.

Driving home from work in his pickup, Jay looked into his mirror. Looking back was the face of a trusted police officer. He smirked. He had the world fooled. Damn, I'm good, he thought.

CHAPTER 11

Two days later, Jay was sitting in front of the TV in his living room drinking a beer. It was almost 11 o'clock at night. He estimated he was on either his fourteenth or fifteenth beer. He needed to lighten up on his drinking a little as he could see the beginnings of a potbelly forming.

Either that, or he needed to work out even more to burn the extra calories he was consuming. Jay had an Olympic barbell set with 300 pounds of weight, a treadmill, and an exercise bike down in the basement. He'd worked out pretty much his entire adult life, so it was really no big deal to think he would have to do just a little extra. Of course, drinking all of this beer was not conducive to maintaining a good workout program. It was easy to find an excuse not to lift or run after he had already drank two, much less a dozen or more beers.

* * *

Angela was already in bed, but he figured she probably was not asleep. She'd blown up with him about an hour earlier about all of his drinking and he had really gone off on her. He felt a little bad about how he'd been treating her. But hey, if she couldn't handle the person that he was, she could just get out and take those kids with her.

The children were increasingly frustrating. He would want peace and quiet and they would be loud and noisy. He expected good grades from both of them, but their last report cards showed their grades had slipped and he'd gone off on them about that.

Jay sat there for several more hours. Just sipping on one beer after another and thinking about the three people he'd killed. Moe Jackson had deserved to die and Jay had no qualms at all about killing him.

Allison was a rich, spoiled brat and he hated people who grew up like that. He couldn't say that he was really pleased with killing her, but he wasn't upset about it either.

Tony was just a punk kid who would have caused more trouble for both the police and for society. Jay had done everyone a favor by killing him. He'd not seen where a missing juvenile report had been filed yet so that meant Tony's mother probably didn't realize he was missing. Society is so fucked up, thought Jay.

On some level, Jay realized what was happening to him, but he really didn't care. He wondered if he would be considered a serial killer yet, but he concluded that he probably wouldn't be. He had not killed enough people just yet.

He had a mission to do and he was the perfect person to do it. He'd always thought the world was overpopulated. If he could selectively reduce the population by knocking off some of the local scum, that was just fine.

Jay decided to sleep on the couch tonight, so he finished off his last beer and got ready to retire for the night. He peeked in his bedroom before lying down, but he couldn't tell if Angela was asleep.

* * *

Morning came early as he woke to pots and pans banging in the kitchen. He rolled off the couch, squinting at the sunlight streaming through the window. Stumbling into the kitchen he yelled, "What the fuck are you doing in here?"

"I'm just cooking breakfast. If you slept in the bed like you are supposed to, maybe you wouldn't hear me."

"You knew I was on the couch. You're intentionally trying to fuck with me," he yelled again. "Why'd you open the curtains when I was lying right there sleeping?"

"Jay, why don't you take a step back and take a good hard look at yourself? The last few months, you've been drinking more and more. You're getting drunk almost every single day. You yell and curse at the kids and me almost constantly." She set the pot down and crossed the room, gingerly touching his arm. "Honey, we love you and we don't like to see you this way."

He could sense the concern in Angela's voice. Maybe he *was* drinking too much. He'd always prided himself on staying in shape and on being one of the top performers at work, but if he kept drinking this much, that was all going to change.

But, everything had already changed. And if he started showing signs of screwing up, that would increase the chances of him getting caught. If he could get himself back under control and reduce his drinking, he'd decrease his chances of getting caught for the murders he'd already committed, and he could continue with his mission.

Jay hesitated for a minute. Then he wrapped his arms around Angela's waist.

"I love you, dear, and I'm sorry. I'll try to cut back on my drinking and I'll try to be better with you and the kids."

He hugged her tightly and kissed her lightly on the cheek. God, his mouth felt like sandpaper again.

Angela looked straight into his brown eyes and stared intently for several seconds. "I want to believe you, I really do, but you need to show me you really are going to change. Show me you're not some alcoholic who just wants to sit and watch TV all night and then I'll start to believe you. Until you do, you are walking on thin ice."

Jay nodded and mumbled that he would try, but he needed her to help him. She told him she would do whatever she could.

Jay's head was still pounding, but he poured himself a cup of black coffee and sat at the kitchen table while Angela continued cooking breakfast. She was making pancakes this morning with cut-up California strawberries in them.

The kids were still in bed. Angela would wake them up and help them to get ready for school in a few minutes, after she'd finished cooking.

You know, I really do have a good family, he thought. I need to be the responsible father that I am. I'll be the savior of the good people and I'll pick off the scum of society one by one.

"What are you smiling about, Jay?"

"I'm just so happy to have such an understanding wife."

"Just don't push me anymore, or you'll find out how understanding I am."

Yeah, that's right, he thought while smiling back at Angela. I'll be mild mannered Officer Jay by day and avenger of the toads by night. If I can get rid of enough of them, I really will make a difference in this town.

Angela brought him a plate of strawberry pancakes. Then she left to wake up the kids. Jay ate slowly, thinking that hangovers are really hell. Maybe he should quit drinking. That would probably help to clear his head and to make him a more efficient killer.

He smiled again as he saw Tim and Marie take a

seat at the table with him. Life is good, he thought. The kids are young and they'll forgive me for my temporary lapse in judgment. They'll tell themselves it was because of Moe and everything will be all right with me.

CHAPTER 12

Jay was off on this cool and blustery day and he had some errands to run downtown at the City Municipal Building. The City Building was an old, four story, brick building. In years past, it had been first a general store and then a bank. The City had bought it a few years ago and renovated as well as enlarged it.

He realized that he hadn't paid his water bill and it was due today. Also, he could pick up a City Sticker for his truck. While there, he figured he'd walk upstairs to see his friend Al and tell him about his episode of falling off of the porch.

Al was fifteen years or so older than Jay, but they were almost like brothers. Jay had known him for years. Among other things, they'd helped each other out on many different household projects.

Al was a huge man. He had an immense belly that shook like a bowl of jelly whenever he laughed, which was often. His hair was white and he had a matching beard to go with it. Many years, Al played Santa Clause as the local mall during the Christmas season. Today, however, he was working his normal job as one of three zoning officers in the city.

"Hey, Al, you'll never guess what I did the other day," said Jay as he entered the Building and Zoning Office.

"Jay, hey, how's life treating you? I haven't seen you in awhile. You doing okay?"

"Yeah, I'm doing pretty good."

Just then, Jay noticed a beautiful woman walk out of one of the offices in the back and into the break room. She had long blonde hair and she had the body of a goddess. He drew a deep breath and asked Al who she was.

"She's our new Inspector. Pretty hot, huh?" Al replied.

"Wow, where did she come from?"

"She used to work in a different office here in Cutler, but our office just hired her. Her name is Lynn. I'm assigned to train her."

Just then Lynn walked up to the counter with a cup of coffee in her hand. Her blue eyes sparkled and her luscious red lips were turned up in a smile.

"Lynn, I'd like to introduce you to an old friend of mine. This is Jay Mundie."

"Hi, Jay, it's nice to meet you," Lynn said while extending her hand.

"Hey there, how are you doing?" Jay answered

while shaking her hand. His hand lingered on hers for a few seconds longer than necessary, but Lynn didn't seem to mind.

"Hey, Jay, you already have a wife," Al jokingly said. Jay blushed a bit, as did Lynn. He couldn't think of a snappy comeback, so he just remained quiet.

After an awkward moment of silence, Al reminded him he had come there for a reason.

"Oh, yeah. Well, remember the deck I built and what you told me when you came out to inspect it?"

"Yeah, I approved it, but I told you to put a railing on it because it was over thirty inches high."

"Well, I never got around to making that railing. The other night, I slipped and fell right off the damn thing."

"You should have listened to me, buddy. You deserve to have fallen," Al said, laughing.

"Yeah, I know. Hell, I may be a bit slow, but I learned my lesson. The next day I'm off I'm putting a railing on it."

"Let me know when you get it done."

"All right, buddy. I gotta be running." He turned to Lynn, who appeared to be lingering over a stack of papers nearby."It was nice to meet you, Lynn. I'll be seeing you around."

"See ya, Jay," Lynn said.

Al shook Jay's hand. "Take care, buddy."

Walking away, Jay turned for one more look at Lynn. God, she's a beautiful girl if I've ever seen one. That smile just lit up her face and those eyes, how they twinkled when she laughed. And that body, she was wearing a tight pair of jeans that she filled out perfectly.

Jay picked up his city sticker and a few minutes later, was walking out to his truck. He was deep in thought. He really wanted to get to know Lynn a little better. But he was also starting to think about his next victim.

Jay reconsidered Richmond and wondered if he should take a scouting trip over there sometime soon. He knew the city fairly well, but he didn't know the rougher parts of town. That would be where he would need to go if he wanted to follow through with finding a Richmond victim.

Jay decided to take a different route driving home than he normally would. He crossed the railroad tracks and drove through a run-down neighborhood. Many buildings had busted windows or boards instead of windows. He noticed quite a few people hanging out on street corners that he recognized as being ones he had dealt with on the job. This neighborhood was in a district that he didn't work too much, but he still knew it fairly well. It had a large Hispanic population and the area was nicknamed Chorillo. Jay didn't know why it was called that because as far as he could tell, it didn't mean anything in Spanish.

It was about 2 o'clock and Christmas break from school was coming to an end. Jay saw quite a few children, all bundled up with coats and hats, playing in the streets and in the alleys. He saw a few females who he figured were some of the mothers. He only saw one Hispanic guy, who was carrying an unopened twelve-pack as he walked toward an apartment building.

"La Tienda Mexicana" was the name of the store he had come from. That meant "The Mexican Store." Jay thought back a few years to when he had been a rookie cop and there were very few Hispanics living in Cutler. Now, there were literally thousands. Most of them were illegal immigrants from Mexico.

* * *

A thought began to grow and fester in the dark recesses of Jay's brain. The local Hispanics pretty much stuck together and were very hesitant to call the police unless it was a dire emergency. They probably thought they would get deported if they called the police. Also, a lot of them were migrant workers or transients. Jay wondered if he were to knock one off, what the chances were that someone would call the police to report it.

When Jay got home, Angela and the kids were still out. He made his way to the basement and began to work out. Forty-five minutes later, he took a break and walked upstairs to get a glass of water. He was sweating like crazy. He hadn't worked out much over the past several months and his body had gotten a little soft. But he knew he'd be back in shape in no time at all.

He kept seeing Lynn in his mind's eye. She had long, blond hair and blue eyes that just sparkled. He thought about how soft her hand had felt, and how she didn't pull away when he was holding it. Jay just had to find out more about this gal.

Jay returned to the basement and worked out for another fifteen minutes. He finished with three hundred crunches, which really made his stomach burn. Shit, a few days of doing this and I'll get rid of the potbelly I was starting to get.

About the time he was finishing up, he heard a car pull into his garage. He knew Angela must be home with the kids. He was going to make up to his family for how he'd been over the past few months. He walked into the garage to greet them.

Tim jumped out of the car first and Jay scooped him up into his arms.

"Dad, you are all wet and stinky, put me down," Tim yelled at Jay.

Jay put him down. As Marie got out, he bent over and gave her a kiss on the cheek. Marie pulled back when Jay was bending over, and Jay wasn't sure if it was because of the body sweat or something else.

Both kids ran into the house and Angela walked around the car and smiled at Jay.

"Honey, you aren't drinking. I'm so relieved."

"I'm not saying I'm quitting, but I'll stop drinking so much. I'm sorry about the way I've been treating you and the kids. I hope you can forgive me."

Angela didn't answer him, but she did give him a hug.

As they walked up the stairs, Angela in front of him, Jay couldn't help but compare her to Lynn. He thought as pretty as his wife was, Lynn had her beat. Yep, he would have to get to know her better.

Also, he needed to figure out how to find his next victim. Just then, another image of Lynn flashed through his mind.

CHAPTER 13

Two weeks later, Jay was working day shift, patrolling the north end of Cutler.

The day had been fairly quiet so far. There had been a minor traffic accident in the morning, but there was less than a thousand dollars worth of damage so he didn't need to make a report. With accidents like this, the responding officer would just have the two drivers exchange information. He would also run status checks on each driver to make sure each one was properly licensed and not suspended or revoked.

Jay had written several speeding tickets, but all in all, it was a slow day. At about 5:30, he was pulling into the parking lot of the PD when he saw Lynn walking to her car. Jay pulled up next to her to say hi. She surprised him by opening the passenger door and asking if she could go for a ride with him.

Jay hesitated for a moment. No civilian could ride with an officer without first getting permission from the Police Chief. He quickly glanced around. Not seeing anyone, he grabbed his duty bag from the passenger seat and told her to jump in. He then pulled out of the parking lot.

Fortunately, it was getting dark already and that meant there was less chance that anyone would see Lynn.

"So, how has your day been?" Jay asked when they were a block away.

"It was pretty shitty actually. That's why when I saw you, I wanted to jump in so that we could go somewhere quiet and talk for a bit. Know any spots where we could sit for a while?"

We're in a marked police car and we do stand out, he thought. Out loud, he mused, "Let me think. There is an old logging trail at Forest View Park. It has a chain across the entrance, but I have a key to the lock. We can go there."

It took a few minutes to get to the park, as it was a two-mile drive. They didn't pass any other cruisers. He pulled up to the rusty chain and got out to unlock it. It was pitch dark here in the woods. Returning to the car, he drove over the chain and then got back out to lock it up so no one would know they were there. This trail went back for several miles, actually going out of the city and into the county.

Jay followed the rough dirt road for about a mile to a spot where he could back off the road. He stopped and parked, but left the cruiser idling.

Lynn had been talking off and on during the ride out here, explaining how bad her day had been. Now that they were here, he looked over and saw a tear glistening on her cheek.

"Hey, what's wrong? Why are you crying?"

"I don't know. It just seems I'm all alone and I really don't know anyone around here." She started twirling her hair a bit while saying this.

"Lynn, come on girl. Lean over here and give me a hug."

The cruiser had some radios stacked in between the seats. They made it a little awkward, but still, she felt good against his body. She surprised him when he felt her turn and place her soft lips against his. Her mouth widened and her tongue felt the way to his.

He responded and the kiss went from being a slow, passionate kiss to being something more intense. He slid his hand from behind her back to around front. She had on a plush sweater. He found her breast and rubbed it gently. She allowed this for a moment, but then placed her hand on his and asked if he could stop.

Jay did. He liked Lynn and didn't want to cross the line with her. However, he leaned back over and exchanged several more kisses. He loved it when he was close to her, seeing her small, upturned nose and the twinkle in her eyes.

Jay glanced at his watch. It was almost 6:30. "Lynn, I have to head back to the PD. The shift ends at seven, and I need to get this car back."

"What are you doing tomorrow?"

"I'm off tomorrow, but if there's any way you could take off early, we could meet up somewhere."

"I've been thinking about taking a day off. Maybe I'll just call in sick tomorrow. If I do, I'll give you a call sometime late morning, if that's okay?"

"Sure, or tell you what, I'll give you a call at 11AM if that's cool. Do you want me to call your home phone or your cell phone?"

"Just call my house, I'll be there."

"Okay," Jay said as he pulled into the parking lot and drove over next to Lynn's Subaru all-wheel-drive wagon. As he pulled up, she hopped out, saying, "Thanks for everything." She blew him a kiss and then got into her car.

Wow, Jay thought. She is a one of a kind girl. She must be fifteen years younger than me. I'm not sure what she sees in an old guy like me, but I might as well enjoy it while I can.

Jay pulled over next to his pick-up truck, took his duty bag and placed it in his truck. He then parked his cruiser in its designated spot and glanced into the mirror. He wanted to make sure he didn't have any lipstick on him or have a look that would attract any attention. He looked fine, just a little tired.

Damn, these shifts sure get long sometimes. At least I'm off tomorrow and maybe I'll be able to go farther with Lynn. She is so hot.

As Jay walked into the PD, his Sergeant called out to him.

"Jay, the shift is short tomorrow. I need you to come in and work. It's overtime and you've been bitching lately about not having enough money, so don't give me any shit about this."

Jay just nodded and said he'd be there. He wasn't happy about it, but he did need the money. What really upset him was that tomorrow might have been the day he would have ended up screwing Lynn, but now, it probably wouldn't be.

He called Lynn on his drive home to tell her that his plans had changed for tomorrow as he had to work.

"Hey girl. Guess what?"

"Jay, what's up?"

"I'm going to have to work tomorrow, so it looks like we won't be able to get together. I'm sorry."

"Jay, how come? I really need to see you tomorrow."

"The shift is short. My Sergeant told me I have to work. There's nothing I can do about it. The shift has to meet minimum manpower."

"Isn't there anyone else that can work instead of you?"

"Lynn, I'm a cop and when they tell me I have to work, I have to. Okay?"

"Okay, I guess I'll see you later then," she sighed.

Jay disconnected, feeling pissed off. Damn it, here was a girl he was pretty sure he could have if he could have seen her tomorrow, but now he had to work and she's being bitchy about it. Who does she think she is? She's not my fucking wife.

Jay was still pissed off when he got home. He didn't say too much to either Angela or the kids. Tim came into his room and reminded him about the chess game he had promised to play with him. Jay angrily stood up, but then Tim, seeing the look on his face, told him to forget about it.

"Tim, I told you this morning that I'd play, so go set up the board."

They played a game of chess and Tim beat Jay fairly easy. Tim had been getting pretty good, and Jay's mind really wasn't on the game, so it was no big surprise that he lost.

"Good game, son. You're going to be the new Bobby Fischer if you keep this up."

Tim was obviously very pleased and his grin was ear to ear.

"Hey, you need to be getting to bed. You have school tomorrow and I have to work. Come on now, get your jammies on and hit the sack," Jay told his son as he gave him a hug.

Jay walked into the bedroom and found Angela. She commented that he seemed to be in a much better mood now than he was when he had first gotten home.

"Well, I was a bit upset about having to work tomorrow on my off day. I really wanted to spend the day working around the house. But, twelve hours of overtime will really be nice."

* * *

They chatted for a few more minutes, but then Jay started yawning and said the long shifts really wore on him. He leaned over to give Angela a quick kiss. Then he stood up and said he was going to bed.

"Ok, honey. I'll be there in a little bit."

"Goodnight. I think I'll be asleep pretty quick," Jay said, while yawning one more time.

CHAPTER 14

"Chief, you wanted to see me?" asked Dave.

"Yes, come in and have a seat. I wanted to ask you about the murder case you are working. How's it coming along?"

"Well, I'm still talking to people. I know a witness will turn up eventually."

"Were you able to find any evidence? Any prints off of the girl, any semen or anything on her?"

"No. It's really strange for a killing like this, but it doesn't appear that she was touched in any manner, besides being murdered."

The Chief and Dave chatted for several more minutes. Chief's phone rang and after he answered, he waved Dave out of his office.

Damn, Chief. He knows we have a chain of command here, but he just calls me in his office when he wants to know something. I'd like to see what would happen if I went straight to him if I had a question about something.

Dave was frustrated. Cutler had had very few homicides over the years he'd worked here. Almost all of them had been solved fairly quickly. They were normally crimes-of-passion murders that were easily figured out.

This one was different though. There was no obvious suspect. Well, there was one. The boyfriend was the obvious suspect. He had argued with the girl and he was the last one to see her alive.

However, his alibi checked our completely. Even so, Jay had taken a DNA sample and a set of fingerprints from him just in case.

But so far, nothing had turned up. There was not a single witness that could be found. No prints were lifted at the scene and the girl was clean. The autopsy showed the first cut, the girl's throat, was the fatal cut. It would have taken several minutes for her to die. The killer must have been impatient as he went on to stab her over and over in the chest. Why?

If it was her boyfriend, a motive should have been figured out by now. However, it wasn't her boyfriend who did it and he couldn't find a single other suspect.

Dave kept thinking someone who was just passing through must have done the murder. Random killings like that were extremely rare, but they do happen. If that were the case, it would take a lucky break for him to be able to solve this one.

There was one other case that had been brought to his attention earlier in the day. There was a missing juvenile case that was starting to look a little funny. It seems Tony White, a fourteen year old, had been reported missing by his mother. Normally, a Detective didn't get a missing juvenile case, but the mother was really throwing a fit about Tony's disappearance.

Dave remembered Tony. He was a kid who had been getting in trouble with the law since he was nine. Dave really thought Tony had just run off and would turn up soon. But, Mom was pitching a fit that she thought something had happened to him. He had been missing for three weeks now.

What could he do? If a kid's missing, and no one has seen him or heard anything about him, what could he do? A statewide BOL had gone out when Tony's mother filed the missing juvenile report. I guess I could send out an Amber alert, but we normally only send those out if there are suspicious circumstances. Tony is probably out partying with his buddies somewhere. I guess I'll check with my Sergeant. when I see her to get her opinion.

It was quitting time. Dave checked around for Sergeant O'Rourke, but she was not to be seen. Shit, I guess I'll just send an Amber alert out. If I don't, and something is wrong, I'll really be in trouble, so I might as well have the Desk Officer send one out.

Fifteen minutes later, Dave was walking out the door. On his way out, he passed Officer Torres coming in. Dave noticed a knife in his pocket and he thought about how the majority of Police Officers carry knives. Nah, no way. There is no way a cop killed that girl.

Even so, Dave thought he would pull up the logs of all the Officers who worked from the time the boyfriend dropped the girl off to when she was found. He *knew* nothing would come of this, but he had to do it anyway. Shit, if he remembered correctly, during the time period of the girl's disappearance and discovery, three shifts had worked. That means 75% of the patrol officers had worked during that time period. Oh, well, I still need to see who was working, just so I know.

CHAPTER 15

The day had started off with a bang. Jay was still pissed that he had to get up at 5:30 in the morning on what should have been a day off and a day where he could have gotten some from his hot new girlfriend.

However, right after roll call and briefing and before he even had time to get his duty bag out to his car, a call came out for three officers. Normally, a two-officer call was the most they ever had and a three-officer call meant something big was happening.

When Jay heard them call three officers, he immediately sprinted to his car to get his duty bag seat-belted into the passenger seat. He'd learned early on in his career to belt his bag in after the first time he was responding to a call and his bag went flying, almost causing him to have an accident.

The call was for a shooting in progress on Fayetteville Avenue. The dispatcher didn't know any more information other than there were several people outside, all allegedly shooting at each other.

Jay was the first out of the parking lot, with his lights and sirens going. Jay was normally a cautious driver, but sometimes he liked to blow the carbon out of his engine as his Sergeant put it, and he would really push his car hard.

Jay was hitting about eighty miles per hour, and he had a green light. He was heading through the intersection. Someone decided to make a right turn on red and they pulled out right in front of him. Jay had no time to hit his brakes, so he swung the wheel hard and he thought his car was going to flip. It didn't and he safely made it around the elderly guy driving the old Chevy Impala.

Whew, that was close, Jay thought while taking a deep breath. He wiped one hand, and then the other on his pants leg to get some of the sweat off.

Jay was slightly shaken up, but what's done is done. Jay shook his head and continued hoofing it to the shooting.

As he swung onto Fayetteville Avenue, he immediately power- braked his car. He swung it sideways. He saw someone outside with what looked like a shotgun. He stopped with his side of the car on the opposite side of where the shooter was.

Jay jumped out of his cruiser. He grabbed his shotgun and took cover to behind the front end of the car next to the engine block. His windshield shattered just as Jay called the other units.

"Shit, get here as fast as you can, but do not turn onto Fayetteville Avenue. We have an active shooter! He just took out my windshield!" Jay screamed into his radio.

Jay heard a popping sound and realized there was another shooter. The second one was on the other side of the street with a handgun. As Jay peeked over his hood, he could see what appeared to be several black males with bandanas on their heads. He saw several Latinos with bandanas hanging out of their pockets.

Gunfire continued intensely, but not at him or his cruiser. Jay smelled the strong scent of gunpowder in the air. He realized that this was a gunfight between the Latino gang MS-13 and the local Bloods. I should have responded slower, thought Jay. If the gangs want to kill themselves, that makes our jobs easier.

Jay peered over the hood of his car again. He saw one young punk turn and take aim in his direction. He heard the gunshot explode. A small puff of smoke came out of the barrel. The gun was pointed in his general direction, but Jay had no idea where the shot landed.

Jay needed more pop than what his Glock could provide. He switched the buckshot out of the shotgun and put in several slug rounds that were mounted on the side of the gun. He kept himself concealed behind the engine block with his Glock in reach while doing this.

Jay visualized what he was going to do. Then he slowly rose up over the hood. He pointed the gun at a young, black punk and pulled the trigger.

He could have sworn he saw a hole opening in the punk's chest. As the guy dropped, Jay turned and fired another slug at one of the Hispanics hiding behind a car. Jay missed the guy, but he hit the side of the car, blowing a pretty good size hole in it.

These two shots had the effect that Jay wanted. He saw several people from both gangs running down the street away from him. Before they reached the corner, he saw two marked units round the corner. The officers immediately jumped out with guns drawn. They ordered the suspects to the ground. All but one dropped immediately. The one who didn't hit the ground made the mistake of raising his pistol up. One officer saw him and pointed his gun toward the suspect. His mouth was moving and Jay knew that he was yelling for him to drop the gun. The suspect kept raising his gun.

Jay saw the officer's gun kick back. The suspect who had the gun was now on the ground, rolling around, screaming in pain. The shot had penetrated his upper thigh.

"What a cluster fuck," Eli said later when he was at the scene. Three people dead, one from a cop and one other who may die, also from a cop.

Jay's cruiser had multiple gunshots in the passenger door and across the hood. The windshield was shattered. Once again, his gun was taken from him, but this time, nobody gave him his. He was allowed to keep his Glock since he hadn't fired a shot from it, but Eli took the shotgun from him.

"Are you doing okay, buddy?" Eli asked.

"I'm fine. I was fucking close to getting shot, but never did."

"Your face is bloody and cut up though. What happened?"

"I think that's from the windshield exploding. I felt the glass hitting me, but I didn't know I was bleeding until now.

"It looks like it's only scratches. But, let rescue take a look at you. And, don't forget to fill out the workman comp forms when you are in the PD just so you are covered."

"Dave will be talking to you again. State Police will do an investigation. You don't have anything to worry about, though. You reacted just like we've been trained to do," Eli said while slapping his back as if congratulating him. "I think if you didn't fire those two shots, we might have had a lot more dead people here."

"Head back to the PD. We're calling in more officers to cover the entire shift. All of you guys need to be debriefed and counseled," Eli said.

Eli called the other officers involved over to him. He told them that once Dave spoke with them, to head to the PD. Dave, other patrol officers and the rest of the detectives would take care of the scene.

Jay was mentally questioning the counseling part, but then he saw Josh, a rookie, sitting on the curbside crying. That fucker needs to toughen up or get out of police work, Jay thought.

Jay watched as his cruiser was towed up on the wrecker. He rode back to the PD with Josh.

"Are you doing okay?" Jay asked the kid.

"I'm not sure. That was the first time I've ever seen a dead person and to know that I almost killed another person, I don't know . . ."

"You were the one who shot the other guy?"

"Yeah."

"Damn, son, don't let that bother you. I saw the entire thing. If you hadn't shot him, someone else would have. If not, either you or your partner would have been shot. You did the right thing."

The rookie didn't respond. Neither said anything else on the ride back to the PD. Upon arriving and getting out of the car, Jay walked around the vehicle and slapped the rookie on the back.

"Hey, you did a good job back there."

The rookie never looked him in the eye.

As Josh walked into the PD, Jay realized, that he didn't even know his last name.

CHAPTER 16

"Josh announced he is resigning tomorrow," Eli told Jay. "He said he was just too shaken up from shooting the guy to continue being a police officer."

"Some people just aren't cut out to be cops. I remember something they told us back in the Academy. You had to make up your mind that if you needed to take another human's life, you would do so without any hesitation. I saw Josh react. He did so without hesitation, but I guess mentally he just wasn't ready to shoot someone," Jay said to several guys standing around.

No police officer in Cutler had shot and killed anyone in twenty years. Then in the span of several months, Jay had killed two people in the line of duty and Josh had shot another one.

Toward the end of the day, Eli called Jay into his

office. He told him, just like last time, he would be suspended with pay while the State Police did an investigation. He again reiterated to Jay that he should take as much time off as he needed.

While driving home, Jay called Lynn and found she was in her office. She'd already heard about the shooting. Shortly after the shooting took place, word spread rapidly around the city Building.

"Yes, I'm okay. I'm heading home now to get cleaned up."

"Are you sure you're not hurt?"

"I'm fine. I just have a few scratches. I'll be off the next several days, though.

"How come?"

"It's normal policy anytime an officer is involved in a shooting, we get several days off. They need to do an investigation to make everything was done correctly."

"Ok. I'm glad you aren't hurt. Can I see you tomorrow?"

"Sure, I'll call you around eleven."

Jay then called Angela at her job. She had already heard as well. Someone in her office told her there had been a shootout and three people were killed. She in turn, had called down to the PD where the desk officer, who knew Angela, told her that Jay was involved and he had killed another person.

"Honey, I'm just fine. This shooting was even more clear-cut than when I shot Moe. There were two gangs fighting. They had already killed two of their own members; they shot up my car pretty good before I even fired my first shot. Don't worry, I'm not in any trouble and I'll be back to work in no time. And no, I'm not going to start drinking again."

* * *

Later that evening, Jay and Angela were sitting in the living room of their house. The kids were in bed, so they were alone.

"Honey, how can you sit there and say that killing this guy doesn't faze you?" Angela asked.

"Because they deserved to be shot. Fuck, that guy today was trying to kill me. What else was I supposed to do? I am never going to hesitate to shoot anyone if I think they are going to shoot me. Angela, as I've told you a hundred times, I'm coming home at the end of the day, no matter what I have to do."

"Jay, I know. But, I'm worried about you. You've now killed two people. How is this going to affect you? You remember what happened last time."

"Angie, I'm not going to start drinking again. Don't worry about me," Jay assured her.

She leaned over and hugged Jay. He embraced her back. His lips found hers and they kissed. Slow, but passionate. Jay finally broke free and stood up. He held her hand and led her to the bedroom. However, once there, Angela told him that she really didn't want to make love. Not tonight, at least, maybe tomorrow.

Jay didn't say anything in response. In a small way, he felt rejected. But, he was really worn out and needed to sleep. And, he did want to keep himself fresh for tomorrow, just in case.

The sun rose the next morning to find a silver coating of frost across Jay's front lawn. He got up first. When Angela arose, she smelled bacon and eggs cooking in the kitchen.

"What's the occasion, dear?"

"I just wanted to make you a good breakfast, honey."

They ate with only a few words of conversation between them. They sat across from each other at the table. Jay kept his eyes focused downward. Angela ate while staring out the window. When Angela left after breakfast with the kids, Jay gave her a kiss and she kissed him back, but something was missing.

Well, that's okay, thought Jay. I'll be seeing Lynn later today. She'll treat me right.

Jay called Lynn at 10:30. Lynn sounded very happy to hear from him. She told him she had taken off and immediately asked him if he could come over today.

"Sure, give me your address."

Lynn told him the address and Jay said he would be over in about an hour.

On the ride over to Lynn's house, Jay realized most of the houses in that neighborhood had parking spots in the back off of the alley. That's good; there is no sense in advertising I'm at her house.

Jay pulled into her driveway off of the alley and parked next to her car. He walked to the door and was raising his hand to knock when the door opened abruptly.

Lynn was wearing a pair of tight cut off denim

shorts and a red halter-top. She smiled shyly at him.

"Isn't it a little cold for shorts?" Jay asked her upon entering the warm house.

Lynn told him that she liked to dress comfortably when she was hanging around her house. She did have some magnificent legs. Jay guessed that she was about 5'8" tall. He also noticed she was wearing heels, which really helped to emphasize those shapely calves.

"Hey, do you want anything to eat or drink?"

"A glass of water will be fine."

They went into the living room and sat on the couch. They chatted for a few minutes and then Lynn started rubbing her bare foot across Jay's leg. This immediately excited him. However, he took it slow at first. He leaned over and kissed her softly on her lips. Her mouth widened and he felt her tongue enter his mouth.

She was going at it pretty fierce and Jay responded accordingly. Their bodies pressed together tightly and Jay's hand was massaging her back. Damn, the girl was just poking right through her halter-top. He slid his hand into her top. He felt her nipple, her soft breasts and the soft brush of her cotton bra.

She did not stop him this time. He softly massaged her breasts. Then, he started to pull her top off. She abruptly stopped him from doing this.

"Don't move so fast, okay?"

I'm a goddamned guy and you get me all fired up and then you stop me. Just like a typical woman, Jay thought.

"I won't do anything you don't want me to do," Jay told her.

They kissed again. He felt her breath on his cheek. His lips nuzzled hers. He softly kissed her cheeks, then her neck. Her lips found his again, her tongue exploring his. He went back to kissing her neck, then her shoulders, then lower. She arched back, allowing him to continue so he went lower until his mouth found that elusive breast.

Lynn allowed this suckling and kissing to go on for several minutes and then she gently pulled him back up. Her mouth found his again, much harder this time. Her hands were rubbing his sides, his back. He felt her hands tugging at her shorts.

At about that time, Jay's cell phone started ringing. Jay looked at the number and saw that it was Eli's office phone number. Jay debated whether to answer it.

"Damn it," he said, clicking the phone on.

"Hey, how are you doing?" Eli asked.

Jay, rubbing Lynn's leg, said, "I'm doing fabulous."

"Great. Can you come down to the PD later on to write another statement? It seems some of the gang members are saying that you and Josh started shooting at them after they had thrown their guns down. We know this is bullshit, but we need to get detailed statements from everyone just to cover ourselves.

"I'll be there in a bit, if that's okay."

"Sure, just make sure you get here before five so we can get your statement taken. You know Dave always wants to get out of here as close to five as he can."

When Jay hung up, Lynn asked him what was happening. Jay explained it to her, while holding her in his arms. He kissed her again and she hungrily responded. They started going at it again and Jay said there was time to go back into the bedroom if she wanted.

Lynn told him "Not just yet. Give me a few more days and I'll be ready for that."

When Jay left there, he was driving away just shaking his head. Damn, this was frustrating as hell. How in the world could that pretty young thing be coming on to him, but then stop in her tracks? He didn't know how girls could do this, but guys could not just turn it off instantaneously.

Jay hoped the next time they got together Lynn would not try to stop him. He might not be able to.

CHAPTER 17

It was three days later, and Jay was back to work. It was his normal graveyard shift and his first day back since the shooting. He hoped the night would be quiet, but then again, a little bit of excitement could be fun.

The last few days had been okay. The shootings were still a hot topic on the news, but even the liberal news media was saying that the gangs had brought it upon themselves. Jay's name was brought up frequently. It was always said he was the one who had killed Moe Jackson back in the fall, but they usually did not elaborate.

Eli had called him just a few hours ago telling him that the State Police had closed their investigation. They had found the shootings by Jay and Josh were both justified. Eli told him to take as much time off as he needed, but Jay responded by saying he would be back into work that very evening. And, so he was.

The night was passing by slowly. Jay had worked a three-car accident earlier in the evening, but it was no big deal. Two cars were stopped at a red light, one behind the other. Then a third car came up and without even hitting their brakes, plowed right into the second car. That car was then pushed into the first car.

The car was only going about 30 mph, but all three cars were messed up pretty good. No one was seriously hurt, so that made it an easy accident to work.

Now, several hours later, Jay was patrolling alongside the river when he spotted a rough looking white man walking. As he passed, the guy turned his head. He had long, scraggly brown hair. When Jay waved, the chap smiled, revealing missing front teeth. Jay did not recognize him, so he decided to check him out.

Jay backed up and got out of his car without notifying EOC.

"Hey, man, where are you headed?" Jay asked him.

"I'm just passing through. Thanks for checking on me, but I'm okay."

"It's cold out here and you aren't dressed very warm. Where are you from?"

"Here and there. I started five days ago in Kansas and I've hitched rides and I've walked and now, here I am."

***

It was cold out, but Jay could still smell him. He was in need of a bath and a shave. A change of clothes would also be nice.

While talking to him, Jay suddenly spotted the butt of a knife sticking out of his belt. Jay pulled his gun and told him to turn around. The guy did so, saying he didn't want any trouble. Jay put his black leather gloves on and then removed the 10-inch knife from his waistband.

"What do you think you're doing? Don't you know it's illegal to carry a concealed weapon in Virginia?"

"It's just a knife, man."

"Any knife with a blade over three inches long needs to be carried in plain sight."

"Aw, come on Officer. I haven't done nothing. Keep the knife, I don't care, but just let me go. I'll leave town and you'll never see me again."

Jay started to feel that urge once again. The drifter was facing away from Jay. Jay took a look around and didn't see another soul in sight. He licked his lips. He felt the weight of the knife in his hand. Moonlight glistened off the sharp, jagged edge of the blade.

It was a cold winter night and the area was deserted. This road was seldom used. There was a thick triple row of pines and then the river. Jay told the drifter to hang tight for a minute.

Jay suddenly plunged the knife as hard as he could into his lower back area, turning and thrusting the blade as it entered his body. The bum let out a small yelp. However that quickly stopped. He fell to the ground, with the knife still sticking out of his back.

In the moonlight, Jay saw blood seeping through his jacket. It appeared that the hilt of the knife was rising and falling, as in synch with his heartbeat.

Jay could see he was still breathing, so he thought about what to do. If he left him, he might not die and could identify Jay. As far as Jay could tell, there was nothing to link this person to him at all. So, he reached down and pulled the knife out.

"Aghh," he wailed in pain.

Jay, using his boot, rolled him over. His eyes were wide open and he whispered, "What are you doing, man? Help me."

Jay thought for just a second. He slowly raised the knife above his head. He asked, "Are you ready to die?"

"No, man. Please."

"Well, this is your lucky day. I'm going to let you live..."

"Thanks, man. Can you call me some help?"

"No. I said I'm going to let you live, but only for a few more seconds."

"Come on . . ."

His voice changed to a yell as Jay plunged the knife into his chest. He gave a final groan. His legs spasmodically twitched a few times. The knife must have hit a rib. Jay heard some cracking and popping. He had to push hard to get the knife to go all the way in. The legs kicked, but then lay still.

Jay stood there, looking down. Then he looked at his hands. His gloves were covered with blood. He even had some blood on his shirtsleeves.

"Fuck!"

Jay decided to drag the body into the pine trees. He was heavier than he looked, but Jay got him into the pines where he wouldn't be seen if someone was driving by, or even if they were walking down the street.

Jay took the knife out of the body and tossed it into the river. The Johnson River was about 100 feet wide and 30-40 feet deep in places. The knife should sink to the bottom and would probably never be found.

Jay went back to his cruiser, opened his trunk and took out a red biohazard bag. He removed his gloves and placed them into this bag.

He took out his alcohol hand cleaner and squirted some on the blood on his shirtsleeves and then took a rag out of his trunk and tried to wipe the sticky blood off the best he could. His uniform was a dark Navy Blue and as long as he got the obvious blood off of him, no one should notice anything at all.

Jay cleaned himself up the best he could, putting the rags in the bag with the gloves. Jay then placed the bag on the passenger side floorboard of his cruiser.

Driving out of there, Jay didn't pass a single other car. That was good. He drove slowly back to the PD and once he got there, he pulled up next to his truck and placed the biohazard bag behind the seat of his truck.

He then walked into the PD and fortunately, did not see anyone else. He went back to the rest room and took a good look at himself. From the reflection in the mirror, Jay felt he looked okay.

He decided he would call another officer to meet with him somewhere, just so he would have an alibi if he ever needed one. Jay called Ben on the radio and they met at the empty city parking lot.

The two friends talked for the next hour. Ben had two young children, both under five, so they talked a lot about kids. Jay, having the older kids, was the more experienced father. He tried to pass on some of his knowledge of children the best he could.

Jay also talked about going into the mountains. He loved the beauty of nature and he loved hiking trails. Jay talked about this for a few minutes, but Ben quickly got bored, as he was more a city type person. Yawning, Ben said he had to go gas up his cruiser, so at 5:45 AM, they both drove away.

At 7 o'clock, Jay was the first one headed out to his vehicle, saying he was tired and had to get home to get to bed.

Once at his house, Jay undressed and placed his uniform in the red bag with the other items. He would dispose of this later on, either by fire, or in the landfill.

He took a shower and then hit the bed. Damn, he thought. How many does that make? I've killed five people and I haven't gotten into any trouble for doing it. Jay smiled. Could life get any better than this? He kept smiling as he drifted off to sleep.

CHAPTER 18

Jay was bone tired. He was working his fourth twelve-hour night shift in a row. During his first graveyard, he had killed that straggler by the river, but he hadn't heard anything about anyone finding his body. That was good. The more time that passed before his body was discovered would reduce the chances that anyone would find any evidence at all linking him to the crime.

This night was passing slowly, just like the past three had. There had been several domestics he had responded to and he had arrested one DUI, but that was about it. It was only one o'clock in the morning, so he still had about six more hours to go until he would get off for the next three days.

Jay knew of a good hideout spot where he could park his cruiser. As far as he knew, he was the only cop to use this location to catch a few winks. Every cop had a spot they would go to if they wanted to hide out to take a nap or just to escape for a little bit. Jay's spot was in one of the parks, off a beaten path that was wide enough for his car to drive into. He'd go back in the woods just far enough to hide his car from view.

The park was off limits at night. However, teenagers and others would sometimes walk through the park. But he never knew of them to wander back that trail, and he really wasn't worried that anyone would ever come upon him. Of course, he always kept his windows down and the radio turned down, so if someone were walking nearby, he would hear them.

Jay pulled into the park and shined his spotlight. There were shadows he couldn't see through. It was spooky, not knowing what may lie in the shadows. He didn't catch sign of anyone else being there. He pulled onto the grassy area and then drove onto the trail and down it 100 yards or so. He was completely out of sight.

Jay sat for a while, just contemplating everything that had transpired in the past few months. He did not have a shred of remorse about killing any of those people. They had all deserved to die for one reason or another.

He thought a lot about Lynn as well. What was going to happen with them? Jay was married, with a beautiful son and daughter. Lynn was a young, hot girl who he was really crazy about. He knew he was going to have her one way or the other.

He was sitting there fantasizing about the various things that he and Lynn would do. Then, he heard something. His senses sharpened. He instinctively placed his hand on the butt of his gun. Voices, it was voices.

Shit, he thought. Jay slowly opened his door and got out. Police cruisers were set up so the interior light would stay off when the door opened, so he didn't have to worry about that. He very softly closed the door, just enough so it barely clicked shut.

It was pitch dark here in the woods, so he knew that he could creep down the bare dirt trail without fear of someone seeing him. Jay started slinking down the trail, heading in the direction of the voices. As he crept, he heard the voices again. He strained to hear them clearly, but the most he could tell it was male's voice and a female's.

After creeping about fifty yards, he could hear them much better. The one voice was definitely a teenage boy's voice. It was deep, but not quite as deep as a grown man. The girl was giggling quite a bit. It sounded like it was a teenage couple that were getting it on or were about ready to get it on. Damn, Jay thought. It may be a warm night out here considering it is the middle of winter, but it's still pretty freaking cold out. They have to be teenagers, as no sane couple would be outside in the middle of the night like this.

Jay estimated they were twenty yards or so ahead of him. In that general area, there were some spots where during the summer, the parks and recreation people would set up some picnic tables for folks to use. During the winter, the tables were removed, so it was a big enough area that some enterprising young people could use it as their bedroom.

Jay tried to imagine what they were doing by the sounds he heard. They must have brought a blanket with them. Even if they were young, crazy and horny, they probably wouldn't be on the bare ground in the middle of winter. Eventually, Jay figured they were in the middle of their lovemaking.

He knew what he was going to do. He licked his lips in anticipation. There were going to be two more to add to his list.

He would walk right up on them and surprise them. They didn't have any idea that he was there. As long as the girl, or even the guy, didn't scream, he would be okay. Jay crept right up to them, and wham, shined his flashlight right on them. Yep, there they were, caught in the act. They still had half their clothes on, probably because it was so cold out.

The boy was on top of the girl. He had turned when the light hit him. He had a look of surprise on his face. The girl had a frozen smile. She reached out and grabbed the corner of the blanket and pulled it over them.

The boy appeared to be about seventeen or eighteen. Jay guessed the girl was younger, maybe fourteen or fifteen. Jay told them he was a police officer and for both of them to get up and put their clothes on. They asked what was going to happen and Jay said that he was going to take both of them home and tell their parents what they had been doing. He kept his powerful flashlight on them so they couldn't see him.

"Sir, please let us leave."

"Quiet. I'm taking you to your parents."

"Please. I promise. No, we both promise, we won't come back here again if you let us leave." The boy was practically begging him.

"My car is right out there in the parking lot. You can follow me home, but please, don't tell my parents."

"I want the two of you to walk to my police car. I'm going to drive you home."

Jay told them his car was parked farther down the trail and he walked behind them, shining his flashlight so that they could see. Both kids were punks, but the girl was kind of cute, even though she was really young.

When they made it to his cruiser, they both got into the back seat as Jay instructed them to do. The girl was sobbing softly. The back seat of his cruiser had a cage. Once they were in, there was no way they could get out by themselves.

Jay started his car. Instead of turning around to drive back into the park, he started driving farther down the trail. The boy asked where he was going. The slide window was closed, so he had to speak loudly to be heard. Jay answered, saying that the trail would come out onto Route 16.

"You two are going to have some fun with me before I take you home."

The trail led into a National Forest, and it eventually ran into an old logging road. Jay knew these old roads like the back of his hand. In years past, he'd supplemented his income by cutting firewood on his days off. Many times, he had worked in the woods here. Since it was a National Forest, he had to have a permit to cut wood there. He always paid the $25 fee. It wasn't much to pay for as much wood as he took out.

The roads went for miles. There were no houses at all out here. The closest was probably ten miles away. Jay also knew that during this time of year, the odds of someone camping out here were slim to none.

Jay knew of a spot about a quarter of a mile off the logging road, where there were some small caves that he'd explored in the past. They didn't go very far underground, but they went far enough that if someone was in them, they were completely hidden.

Jay thought about how he had never seen anyone in or near these caves. It would be the perfect spot to take care of business.

The radio had been quiet for the past two hours. If he were to get a call, he wasn't sure exactly what he would do. However, luck continued to be on his side as not a sound was heard from the radio the entire time he was out there. The entire shift was tired and everyone was probably taking a nap somewhere or another.

Jay pulled over and sat for a minute before getting out. Sobs could be heard from the back seat. He shut the car's lights off. It was pitch black. He knew exactly where the caves were. He knew what the final outcome was going to be. He decided to take the kids out one at a time, as it would be easier that way.

Getting out of the car, he pulled his gun out and opened the driver's side door of the back seat. The boy was sitting on that side. Jay told him to get out, while holding his Glock down at his side.

The kids looked terrified. They immediately started begging to be let go. The girl was sobbing and it looked like the boy was also. Once the boy was out, Jay slammed the door shut.

The boy asked him where they were going. Jay told him that he would see soon enough.

Jay grabbed the boy by his arm.

"Put your hands behind your back."

When he did so, Jay handcuffed him.

They made it to the cave. Shrubs were in front of the small entrance. Jay pushed the boy through, hearing the boy's screams as the branches scratched him. The boy stumbled once on a rock and Jay let him fall. Jay grabbed him and yanked him back up.

Once there, Jay had the boy go about twenty feet into the cave. It was pitch black, with the only light coming from the Mag-Lite that Jay was holding. Jay told the boy to stop walking and to sit down on a large rock. The boy did so, crying steadily, shoulders shaking. Jay kept the light shined on him, blinding the boy to what Jay was doing. Jay had re-holstered his gun while they were walking and had pulled his knife out of his pocket.

As the boy was sitting there crying, Jay walked behind him. He suddenly grabbed his hair and pulled his head back. The boy's yell was cut off and suddenly changed to a gurgling sound. Jay's right hand had brought the knife down. He slashed him across the throat. Blood spurted out, but Jay was ready for this and had stepped back immediately after slashing him. The boy fell over on his side, making small gurgling sounds as the blood pulsated out. It didn't take long at all until the flowing blood came to a stop. By then, Jay knew that the boy was dead.

Being careful not to get blood on himself, Jay rolled the boy onto his side where he could remove the handcuffs. No blood was on them, so he placed them back in his handcuff case.

Jay walked out of the cave and went back to his cruiser. When he arrived, he found the girl crying and banging on the windows. Jay yanked the door open. He reached in and grabbed the girl and pulled her out. She screamed hysterically. He backhanded her across the face. This didn't shut up her crying, but it took the fight out of her. Her nose was probably broken. It was dripping blood.

The girl was still crying softly. Jay cuffed her as well with her hands behind her back. They walked without talking, the only noise being the sobs coming from the girl and the scuffling of their feet.

CHAPTER 19

Jay and the girl made it to the entrance of the cave and the girl stopped. He had gagged her with an old rag from the trunk of his cruiser after cuffing her. He knew no one could hear her, so he loosened her gag. He wanted to hear her beg.

"Please, please, don't hurt me," she cried out.

Jay immediately smacked her and stuffed the gag back into her mouth. That was more than enough for him. He wasn't in the mood to listen to any whining.

"Get in there," he said as he pushed her. She fell, but he grabbed her from behind. He didn't want her to hurt herself.

She made her way into the cave. It was tight at the entrance and they had to duck down to get in. However, once inside, they could stand fully upright.

Jay was shining the light for them as they walked. He was careful to not shine it on the boy.

Once they were inside and back a little ways, Jay told her to stop. She asked where Tom was. Jay said he was tied up close by, but that he had a rag in his mouth so he couldn't talk. Jay was curious as to what the girl's reaction would be if she saw her boyfriend, so Jay decided to shine the light on Tom for her to see.

When he did so and the girl saw Tom lying there in a pool of blood with his eyes wide open but unseeing, she tried to scream. Jay could see the fear in her wide eyes. She was trembling and turning red from her effort. She appeared to be on the verge of really freaking out. Jay started laughing at her helplessness. Jay had expected her to react like this, but what happened next he did not expect.

She bolted, trying to get past Jay. This surprised him, but he still reacted before she got past him. He grabbed her and she started kicking. She caught his shin with one of her kicks. Jay grunted in pain, which pissed him off even more.

Jay threw her back as hard as he could. She was very unsteady, partly due to her hands being cuffed behind her back. Jay watched her fall back. He saw at the last second what was going to happen. He lunged for her, but couldn't catch her. She fell hard. She hit head first, directly on the edge of a sharp rock.

Jay was breathing hard as this had really surprised him. He was ready to kill the girl right then and there. However, when he looked at her, she had a small line of blood trickling down her face. She was not moving.

Jay checked her pulse. She was dead. This was not how he had wanted it to end. He wanted to cut the girl's throat, just as he did with the boy. He screamed out in frustration. He had missed out on the pure pleasure in taking this girl's life. He felt cheated.

He took the cuffs off the girl and placed them into the case. Shining the light around, he looked to see if there was any evidence that could be used to identify him. He didn't think so. He wondered if the cuffs could have caused any bruising that could be detected, but he doubted it. If the cuffs had been really tight or if she had struggled a lot, maybe she would have some bruising. But he hadn't put the cuffs on that tight and she had died before a struggle had really ensued.

Jay walked back to his car and got in. He drove down the logging road, thinking that it was very good that there was so much rock. His tires would not leave any marks on this road. It had been so cold that even on the bare ground, he probably wouldn't leave any footprints as it was still partially frozen.

Jay made it back to the park in about ten minutes and then made his way down the trail. When he was still fifty yards or so away from the park, he stopped, shut his car off and listened. Not hearing anything, he decided to walk the last fifty yards just to make sure no one was there before he drove his marked cruiser out of the trees.

Jay glanced at his watch. It was 3:30. He still had

not heard a sound from his radio. Getting to a point where he could see into the park, Jay softly cursed. There was a vehicle there. He squinted, trying to see if anyone was sitting in it. He stood there in the shadows, watching, waiting. He saw no movement from the car.

Then, it hit him. This had to be the kid's car. He had forgotten all about the boy telling him his car was parked here.

Jay walked back to his cruiser and got in. He drove into the park. He went past the car, making a note of the car's tag. Then he drove out of the park and started making his rounds, checking businesses.

While doing so, he thought about that car being there. He didn't know anything about those two kids, but he figured it wouldn't take too long until one of their parents or both sets of parents called the police, reporting them missing. When that happened, if the car hadn't already been logged as being in the park, it would probably be quickly discovered.

Once the car was found, what would happen? Would Dave and the other officers think that someone had picked them up in a different vehicle, or would they work it as the kids had walked away from the car?

Jay had probably driven twelve miles or so away from the park and once off of that trail, there were multiple different logging roads that intersected each other, crisscrossing through the forest. All together, there must be hundreds of miles of these roads.

Jay figured as long as no one found any evidence of the kids being on that trail, that he would be safe.

Shit, shit, shit, Jay almost screamed it. The kids had been lying on a blanket when they were screwing and he had never picked it up, so it would still be there. Once that was found, that would tell the whole fucking world that the kids had been on that trail and that would get everyone looking harder in the area.

Driving back toward the park, Jay noticed it was 4:15 in the morning. There were still a few more hours of darkness left.

He would go back there, parking as close as he could to the trail, without leaving the parking lot. He could then run down the trail, pick up the blanket and anything else that might be lying there and get it into his car and get the hell out of there.

When he was only two miles away, Jay heard his radio crackle.

"89 to EOC, 10-28, 29 through Virginia."

That was John running a tag on a car. A 10-28 was requesting EOC to run the registration of the car and a 10-29 was a wanted check, to see if the car was entered as being stolen. EOC was dispatch, the Emergency Operations Center.

"EOC to 89, go ahead."

John gave the plate number to EOC. Jay realized at once this was the tag of the kid's car.

Shit, John must have driven through the park and found the car sitting there all alone. It was common to run a tag like that. If it weren't stolen, normally the officer would just tell EOC to log the vehicle in that area. Jay felt himself break into a sweat. Would John get out to check on the car or would he just log it?

Jay turned away from the park, trying to figure out what to do.

"89 to EOC log the vehicle as a dark Toyota two-door. It's parked here in the park."

Jay had to think for a minute. Then, picking up his microphone, he called John.

"77 to 89," Jay called.

"Go ahead."

"Can you 10-25 me at the old Wilco station?" This station was closed. It was located on the opposite of the city from the park.

"10-4, but I'm still in the park, so it'll take me a little while to get there."

"10-4, I'll check a few more businesses than meet you there."

Jay waited about two minutes. He figured that was plenty of time for John to get out of the park. He drove slowly in that direction. He would literally shit his pants if he was going in and John passed him. He stopped two blocks away and waited another two minutes. He was safe, John was nowhere around.

Jay parked his car. He ran back to where the kids had been. Shining his light, he looked around. He didn't see anything at first. He felt the panic starting to rise and then, he saw it. There was an old blanket spread out. He rolled it up and giving a second look and seeing nothing, he went back to his cruiser and placed the blanket in the trunk.

Twisted Obsession

He then headed out and went to meet John. John was already there when Jay pulled up. Jay told him he'd been checking a few doors and took longer than expected.

They chatted for a while and both guys started yawning. It was now about 5:15 AM. Both were tired and ready for some time off. John finally said he had some more business checks to make so he drove away.

Jay then drove to the Police Department. He saw no one outside, so he pulled up to his truck. He took out the blanket and put it behind the seat in his truck.

He then headed back out and didn't return to the PD until it was almost 7 o'clock and quitting time. Once again, Jay left in a hurry, saying he was tired and he needed to get home to get to sleep.

Upon arriving at his house, Jay decided that leaving the blanket behind his seat was probably the best thing to do for now. He still had a pair of gloves and a uniform back there, but he would get rid of the stuff at the landfill sometime in the next couple of days, before he had to go back to work.

CHAPTER 20

Jay slept all day and didn't wake up until Angela got home from work around 5:30. When she walked through the door with the two kids, he finally struggled to open his eyes. When he saw what time it was, he jumped out of bed, pissed at himself.

Normally, after the last night of working a graveyard shift, Jay would try to get up by noon or one PM. This was the downside to rotating shifts as he had to transition between working twelve-hour nights and twelve-hour days.

When he got up at noon or one PM, this normally meant that he was extremely tired for the rest of that day, but then he would be able to get to bed somewhat early and then get up even earlier the next day. This helped him to transition back to working the day schedule.

However, by sleeping until fucking 5:30 in the evening, now he would be awake for half the freaking night and that meant he would have to cut his sleep short the next night. This made it harder to transition back to day work, but also and more importantly, he was planning to see Lynn during the day and he didn't want to be tired when he saw her.

Angela could see that Jay was upset and she knew why. Jay had been a cop for as long as they had been married and the one thing he hated was transitioning between working nights and working days. He was a guy who thrived on a normal sleep schedule and this shift-work screwed with him a bit.

"I going to get dinner started," Angela said. "Kids, go down to the basement and play."

While cooking, she attempted to have a conversation with Jay, but he wasn't really in the mood.

His mood seemed to improve after he ate his dinner, which was actually breakfast for him. He actually started telling her about how little activity they'd had during the past few nights.

"Well, that's good, isn't it, honey? When it's quiet, then there's less chance of you or any of the other officers getting hurt."

"Yeah, in one way it's good, but in another way, we all thrive on action and excitement. We need to have something happen to help us keep going."

Angela could never understand this need for an adrenalin rush. Initially, she was worried when he worked nights, as she never knew what would happen. Over the years, she never really got used to him working this kind of schedule, but she did come to accept it.

After dinner, Jay told Angela he was going to run to the store to pick up some beer. If he was going to stay up half the night, he might as well have a few beers to drink, as this would probably help him to get to sleep just a little bit faster.

Jay came back with a case of beer.

"What, are you going to have a fucking party or what?"

"The case was on sale. You know money has been tight. Sheesh."

By the time Angela said she was going to bed at 10:30, Jay was on his fourth beer. He really wasn't in the mood to get drunk. He was just in a mood.

As the clock struck midnight, Jay opened his seventh beer of the night. Even though he'd slept all day, he felt pretty tired. He would go to bed when he finished this last beer. That was good, as he wanted to get up by a decent hour.

Lynn had told him she was going to take the afternoon off and he was planning to meet her once she called him.

Jay crashed at 12:30 on the couch. He figured when Angela and the kids got up, his being on the couch in the middle of things would probably help to wake him up. If he was in the bedroom, he might never hear them and would just keep on sleeping.

* * *

Sleeping on the couch worked as Jay started to wake up while Angela was telling the kids to brush their teeth. He forced himself out of bed and staggered to the kitchen to get a cup of coffee. God, he felt rough. A combination of beer with insufficient sleep really hurt. However, if he didn't do this, by the time he had to get up at 5:30 the day after tomorrow to go to work, he'd really be tired. He'd rather be a little tired on a day off than to be tired while working.

Jay was lazing around the house in the morning, just drinking coffee and reading the newspaper. He went and shaved and showered late in the morning. He made some soup for lunch and then at 12:30, his phone rang.

It was Lynn. "Hey, I'll be home in 15 minutes. Come on over."

"Sure, I'll be there in twenty minutes."

After hanging up the phone, Jay splashed a bit of cologne on his face and then locked up and headed out. He pulled up to Lynn's house to see Lynn disappearing inside. She must have just arrived herself.

Lynn yelled back she was going to change into something more comfortable and told Jay to help himself to anything he wanted. Jay just poured himself a glass of water. His throat was still pretty dry.

When Lynn came back out, she was wearing a pair of tight shorts and a t-shirt that was cut off at mid-riff. God, she was beautiful. Jay walked over to embrace her. As he did, he felt her heart beating.

Her soft breasts pushed against him. He leaned over. Their lips met.

Lynn kissed him back and then lightly pushed him away. "Hey, I heard two kids were missing under possible suspicious circumstances. Have you heard anything about this?"

"No, what did you hear?"

"Al had been talking to some cop who said that a seventeen-year-old boy and a fifteen-year-old girl were both missing. Their car had been found in the park and was actually logged there by a police officer the other night. Al said it seemed very suspicious and that both families were very concerned about the whereabouts of their children."

"Do you know anything else about what happened? Who are the teens? Did Al say if we had any leads?

"That's really all I know. I hope nothing bad has happened to them. Is everything okay? You look worried."

"It always concerns me when young people are missing under suspicious circumstances. It's a crazy world we live in."

"It is, but you provide a little bit of sanity for me. Come here and give me a hug," Lynn told him.

They embraced and just held each other for a few minutes. Lynn finally pushed back, telling Jay that she was hungry and she was going to grab a bite to eat.

"Do you want anything?"

"No thanks."

She walked into the kitchen and got out an apple

and a little bit of peanut butter. She reached over to the corner of the counter top where she had a knife rack and she pulled out a small kitchen knife and used that to slice up the apple.

While doing this, she was happily talking with Jay about her morning. She finished the slicing of the apple and after pouring a glass of juice she walked into the living room. She ate the apple slices after first putting a bit of peanut butter on each piece. She told Jay that she tried to eat healthy and an apple with a bit of peanut butter was a very healthy lunch.

Personally, Jay thought a meal wasn't complete without some sort of meat, but that was just him. Looking at Lynn's body, he realized that she must have been doing something right.

After she finished eating, Jay slid over next to her and put his arm around her. She leaned back into him and tilted her face towards his and they started to kiss again.

"You taste like peanut butter," Jay jokingly said after they finished up one long kiss.

"But you like it, don't you?"

"I sure do. Let me taste it again," he said as he started kissing her again.

Their kisses grew more passionate and Jay wondered how far she would let him go this time. His hand went to her flat belly and he started rubbing her stomach and would slowly slide his hand up and touch her breasts briefly, but then he'd bring his hand back down. He had done this several times, when she grabbed his hand and guided it back up under her t-shirt. She wasn't wearing a bra and she felt so warm and inviting to him.

Lynn then pulled her shirt off and told Jay he could enjoy her breasts, but not to go any further. Jay was having fun, but he really wanted to do a little more. However, he realized that Lynn was slowly allowing him to go a little further and if he didn't push her too hard, she would probably let him go all of the way very soon. It had better be soon, he thought.

So, as much as this pained him to do, he settled with kissing and caressing her all over her face, neck and breasts. His hands did venture down below her waist once or twice, but he was just rubbing and not really trying to do much. He could tell that her rear was tight and firm. She really had a killer body and he was so glad he was the one getting the opportunity to experience it, even though it was taking a lot longer than he would have preferred.

This went on for several minutes. Jay knew Lynn was really getting into it. She was moaning softly and was rubbing him all over his chest. Finally, Jay felt her hands go to her shorts, and she unzipped them and pulled them off. Although this surprised him, he knew just what to do. He took it slow and easy. They stayed on the couch for several minutes, but then Jay asked her if she wanted to go to her bedroom. Lynn agreed.

Their lovemaking might have started off slow and easy, but it got harder and faster as they went along. Jay had not felt a power like this ever in his life and the entire experience was absolutely breathtaking to him.

After they finished, both of them were completely exhausted and they dozed off for a little bit. Lynn awakened first, because Jay woke up to Lynn kissing him. She wanted to do it again, but Jay said it was getting late. He needed to get cleaned up and get back home.

Jay asked if it was okay for him to take a quick shower. Lynn told him where to find a towel to use. While showering, Jay thought about what had just happened and wondered how much longer this would go on. He knew it was wrong, but it felt so good.

It was almost 4:30 in the afternoon when Jay said he was ready to head home. Lynn had showered as well and was wearing a bathrobe. Her hair was still wet from the shower. She looked so fresh and beautiful that he couldn't resist embracing and kissing her again. After a long kiss, he rubbed her cheek and told her he hoped to see her again soon.

Jay got back to his house just a few minutes after five. That was perfect timing, because when Angela got home, she would never realize that he had been gone.

CHAPTER 21

It was a beautiful, sunny and unseasonably warm spring day. Jay was thinking about how he'd like to find another victim. The joy that he got from killing someone was immeasurable. It did not compare with any other feeling that he had ever experienced.

Well, the feeling he got when he was around Lynn was close, but even that feeling did not compare with how he felt when he snuffed out another life. He had come to enjoy using a knife to do the deadly deed.

With each new victim, Jay had become more confident in his abilities. After taking the life of his latest victim, Jay thought he was invincible. And as a cop, he knew the ins and outs of how to cover his tracks.

He'd made various mistakes with some of the murders. With that first girl, he'd had his cruiser parked out on a street where anyone could have seen it. But no one did.

* * *

With the kids in the park, he had almost forgotten their blanket and he did forget that they had a car parked in the parking lot. The two bodies were found just last week, almost three months to the day after he'd killed them. As far as he could tell, Dave and the other investigators did not have any clues as to who committed these heinous crimes.

Today on this special glorious day, he took the life of victim number eight. She was a 19-year-old college student, a blonde with blue eyes and a figure that guys would die for.

Jay had decided to do something with her that he'd not done previously. He had sex with her prior to killing her.

He'd met this girl on his last night shift. She was drunk and Jay could have arrested her for being drunk in public, but he didn't. He told the girl, Janice, that if she would give him her phone number and go out with him one time, he would give her a ride home and not charge her.

The young slut readily agreed. Jay walked her up to her apartment, where she volunteered that she lived alone. While there, he asked if he could kiss her. She went crazy kissing him; he had to pull her off of him. He was still on duty and he didn't want to spend too much time logged off at this girl's apartment.

However, he had called her the next afternoon. Jay wasn't sure how the girl would react when she was sober, but she seemed very happy to talk with him and had agreed to meet him today.

Jay told her that he couldn't be seen in public with her. He asked her if she liked hiking in the mountains and she did, so they went to a seldom-used trail that he knew about up in the mountains.

Jay carried a backpack and in the pack, he had a small, thin blanket. When they got about a mile down the trail, there was a side trail that Jay knew would take them to a clearing near a stream. It was a beautiful spot and he knew if he wanted to have the best chance at making love with Janice, he needed to provide the right mood for it.

When they got to the sunny clearing, Jay pulled out the blanket, unfolded it and placed it on the ground. Then he pulled out a bottle of wine and a little bit of marijuana he'd taken from some punk kid a few nights ago. Janice appeared surprised when he pulled the weed out. She said she didn't think cops would smoke weed.

Jay assured her he was not the typical cop. He proceeded to roll up a joint, lit it and took a big puff before passing it to Janice. They handed it back and forth, each inhaling mightily and holding it for a few seconds.

He followed that up by opening the bottle of wine. After taking a swig straight out of the bottle, he handed it to Janice, who did the same.

After several drinks, Jay started kissing Janice. He thought she would devour him. He pulled her t-shirt off. She pulled her pants off. Lynn had a beautiful body, but Janice had the body of a goddess. He kissed her up and down her body.

She kissed him back. She started rubbing him. He did the same with her. This continued for several minutes. Then, it was time. Before Jay entered Janice, he made sure that he put a condom on, as he did not want to leave any evidence.

His plan was never to have the body found; but just in case, he wanted to make sure he didn't leave any clues behind.

Their lovemaking was exquisite. She left him completely worn out. They both dozed for a few minutes, but Jay awakened first. Looking at Janice lying there, Jay knew it was time. He rolled over and picked up his knife, which was still in his pants pocket.

Then, rolling back over, he started kissing Janice. She awoke and started kissing him back. Her tongue began to explore his mouth, even before her eyes were open. He was enjoying this immensely, but he could hold off no longer. While kissing, he reached in between their necks and slit her throat. It was as simple as that. Sure, Jay got blood all over himself, but he didn't care.

Janice started sputtering upon having her throat slashed, so Jay had proceeded to stab her several times in her chest area. He lost count of how many times he had stabbed her.

There were several reasons why Jay brought Janice here to kill her. First of all, he knew this side trail was rarely used. Once the plants started growing, the trail would quickly get covered up and probably no one would walk it all summer.

Also, down from the stream was a small cave. Why not? Jay had left the two teens in a cave and it had taken months for them to be discovered. And with those two, their car had been found so eventually volunteers and police had searched the surrounding area.

Janice was still lying on the blood soaked blanket. He pulled a hatchet from his backpack and held her left hand in his. This was the hand she had used to caress his face while she was kissing him. Now, he would have this memory forever.

Jay was used to cutting firewood and he kept a sharp blade on his small hatchet. One stroke was all he thought it would take. However, it took two. With the second hack, he heard the bone snap. Now Janice's hand was his. The sunlight glistened off a ring she had on her small finger. Jay set the hand upright so any blood that was in it would drain out.

Jay then wrapped up Janice's body in the gray wool blanket and dragged her to the cave. The hole, like a lot of caverns, had a very small opening and was hard to see if you didn't know it was there. However, once inside, the grotto opened up into one of the larger ones that Jay had ever been in. It must have been the size of a two-car garage.

He had no idea how far down the opening went, but Jay dragged Janice for what seemed to be several hundred yards. He was wary of snakes, as he heard a few rattles from time to time. The last thing he needed was to get bit by some rattlesnake while down in this cave with a dead body.

Jay located a small culvert, which would make an appropriate spot for Janice's final resting place. He placed her body into this ditch, unrolling her from the blanket as he did so. He then gathered up enough rocks to cover up her body.

Her eyes were still open, staring. He also noticed her inner thighs were glistening. What memories he had. He figured it could be years until anyone came in here, but then again, it could be only days. He really didn't know. He covered Janice up with rocks and dirt. Her pretty eyes were the last part of her body he covered up.

CHAPTER 22

Dave was sitting at his house, thinking about the two dead kids. The evidence so far was scarce, but he had a feeling. His feelings usually turned out to be right. In this case, he hoped he was wrong.

Thinking back a few months, he had checked the shift schedules after the one girl had been found murdered in an abandoned building. He had a list of officers who had worked during the days when the murder could have occurred.

However, he really didn't consider any of them suspects. That case, so far at least, remained open and unsolved.

Now, he had two murdered teenagers on his hands, a seventeen-year-old boy and his fifteen-year-old girlfriend. Two families were wracked in grief. It was his job to figure out who had done it.

Twisted Obsession

He had gotten the autopsy reports back already. The boy died from loss of blood, due to his throat being sliced. The girl died from a ruptured blood vessel in her head. This occurred from her hitting her head on a sharp rock.

The only other clue that he had was that both victims had injuries on their wrists. These injuries were consistent with the victims having had handcuffs on. This alone, did not lead him to believe that a police officer was behind the killings. However, with the lack of evidence in three homicides, he had to at least entertain the thought that it could be a cop behind these murders.

He knew all the officers in his department. He knew some better than others. He had a tough time thinking one of his brothers in blue could be a cold-blooded killer.

There was no direct evidence leading him to believe that it was a cop behind this. It was a hunch at this point.

Of course, if it was a police officer behind these three homicides, it could be one from a neighboring department. The county surrounded the city and they had their own Sheriff's Department.

He could not get the faces of the teens out of his mind. When they were first reported as being missing, he thought maybe they had run off together. However, as time went on, he and everyone else started thinking there was a good chance foul play had occurred.

It was confirmed when a hiker discovered the bodies in a cave. The bodies had been there for several months. Probably, ever since the night they disappeared. The bodies had decomposed and had been partially eaten by animals.

Autopsy reports showed that neither one had been sexually molested prior to their deaths. There was DNA evidence linking the teenage boy having had sex with the girl, but no one else had.

This case was all that he had thought about for the past few days. He was a good detective. First, the murdered girl last fall had baffled him, now these two kids. He had no evidence connecting the murder of the girl with the teens, but his gut told him they were linked.

He had a list of the officers who worked the night the teens disappeared. He also had a list of the county deputies who worked. He was working on getting a list of the deputies who worked during the time that the other girl was killed.

He really hoped his looking into other law enforcement officers was futile. But, he had a job to do. He had to look into every possible lead. Everyone was a suspect until he proved that they didn't do it.

* * *

He had already interviewed the families of the two teens several times. He was going to talk to some of them again. He was still trying to track down all of their friends. With them being teenagers and in school, they had a lot of friends. His hope was that someone would be able to tell him something that would point him in the correct direction.

Dave was thinking about all of this when something else came to mind. Jay was a good friend of his. However, he had killed twice in the line of duty over the past six months. This was highly unusual for two separate line-of-duty killings to have occurred this close together by different officers. But, but the same officer, it was almost unthinkable.

However, Jay had been justified each time. He was highly regarded in the Department. There was no way Jay could be the killer.

But, there it was, right in front of him. Jay's name was on both lists. This really didn't mean anything. But it was starting to nag at him. He was going to have to take a closer look at Jay.

CHAPTER 23

Jay now had two blankets stuck behind the seat in his Ford pickup. One was in a red biohazard bag he'd taken from the PD. That was the one saturated with Janice's blood. He also had a pair of bloody gloves in there. He really had to get rid of these and fire would be the best way to destroy them.

However, for today, he was going to see Lynn. It was Saturday and it has been almost three weeks since he had killed Janice. During those three weeks, Jay had kept Janice's hand up in the attic where it got pretty hot. His attic always got much hotter than the outside temperature in warm weather. He didn't know what would happen, but the hand was drying out pretty well. It was shrinking up and had gotten very wrinkly.

He had checked on it every few days while it had

been up there. He only went up there to look at it when Angela and the kids weren't home. It amazed him how quickly the hand had become mummified. Her ring, which did fit her finger tightly, now just slipped off. The odor wasn't really that bad. There were attic fans that pulled the hot air out of the space. It pulled the odor of rotting flesh as well.

He wished he could hang this from his truck's rear view mirror, but he thought that might be a bad idea. However, maybe in a few more months, he could figure out a way to preserve the hand. Maybe he'd say he got it at some county fair and people would believe him.

Angela had taken the kids and gone to the park with her parents. They would stay gone for hours. As soon as they left, Jay placed a call to Lynn. She answered on the second ring. He told her he was leaving to head to her house.

* * *

She met him at the door wearing some sexy lingerie she said she'd ordered from Victoria's Secret.

Their lovemaking ranged from slow and easy to hard and intense. Their bodies were in tune together. At times, it seemed they couldn't get enough of each other. But, they both liked it that way and Jay swore that each time he made love to her, it just got better and better.

After their lovemaking, Lynn made him a late lunch of tomato soup and two grilled cheese sandwiches.

"I told you before, I like to eat meat with lunch and dinner," Jay told her.

"You eat too much red meat. Cheese has the protein you need and the soup has some good vitamins."

Jay was hungry, so he ate up without any further conversation. Damn, Lynn sure was beautiful, but sometimes, she fucking reminds me of Angela the way she talks to me, he thought.

Lynn took a shower after lunch. Jay used the opportunity to get the evidence, the blankets, gloves and biohazard bags out of his truck. He figured he'd stash the stuff in Lynn's basement for a few days. She'd never find the shit. It would give him a few days. He would get it all soon and go burn it somewhere.

He put the bags in different spots. He kept the two blankets together. He left the gloves in one bag all by themselves and stashed them behind the washing machine, back in a corner.

The blankets he put in a big chest, underneath a bunch of old clothes.

It was around 3 o'clock in the afternoon when Jay left Lynn's house. On his way back home, he stopped at the hardware store and picked up a washer for the cold-water side of his shower faucets.

Jay made it home and had the shower fixed and was putting his tools away when Angela and the kids came home.

"Hey, honey, we're home," Angela said while walking into the kitchen. "Kids, take your shoes off and set them outside the front door."

"Hi, what did the kids get into to get their shoes so muddy?" Jay asked, walking into the kitchen and seeing his kids taking off their mud-covered shoes.

"They got into the creek and got their shoes all wet when I wasn't watching them and then started playing in some of the mud puddles. I told them that they were too old to be doing that, but they were having a great time."

"Well, that's their school shoes, so they better get them cleaned up."

"Jay, you should have come with us today. You would have had fun."

I did have fun fucking Lynn while you and the kids were out playing, he thought. He wondered how much longer he was going to put up with Angela and the kids. He thought more and more about moving out on his own. He knew that he would, but he had to find the perfect time.

He had now killed eight people, but how many more were to come? Shoot, he had learned so much from killing these first eight that he now thought that he could keep on killing without fear of being caught.

Angela was in the kitchen getting dinner ready and the kids were in the basement playing a video game, so Jay kicked back in his recliner to think a bit.

Who would be his next victim? Killing people was so easy when you knew what you were doing, but he still got such a thrill out of it. Thinking back on all of his victims, he realized that he preferred killing women to killing men and he liked using a knife to do it.

Hmm, maybe I can start specializing in killing women. I've done pretty well with hiding the bodies, but maybe I can start leaving them where they will be found. Some of the famous killers would even leave their own calling card with each body. I need to think of something unique to do.

Jay awoke when Angela started calling everyone for dinner. They were having spaghetti with turkey meatballs and homemade tomato sauce. They also had a salad made of romaine lettuce, sliced onions, cucumbers and cherry tomatoes. He had a beer with his dinner, a bottle of Samuel Adams Winter Ale that he found stuck in the back of the fridge.

The kids were talking about the upcoming baseball and softball season. Jay got tired of listening to them, so he finally picked up his plate and went into the TV room. Angela hated when he did this, but she had tired of complaining to him about it, which he was glad of.

Five beers later, having now started on the twelve-pack of Rolling Rock, he turned his head as Angela came walking in.

"Jay, you told me you were cutting back on drinking. Now you're drinking just as much as ever," Angela said.

"Angie, girl, just fuck off, okay? If I want to drink, I will. I don't beat you like a lot of guys beat their women and I pretty much let you do what you want. I work a good job and I take care of you and the kids, so why do you keep nagging me about drinking?"

"Because when you drink, you talk like this and start cussing out me and the kids. You can't keep doing this, I won't accept it." Her voice shook with conviction. When he didn't respond, she stormed out of the room.

Jay got up at the same time, but instead of following Angela, he walked into the kitchen, draining his green bottle of Rolling Rock as he walked. He opened another bottle and stepped onto the deck.

It was still chilly at night, even though the days were beginning to warm up a bit. It was pushing 11PM. Jay had to work daylight shift tomorrow, so maybe he'd finish this beer and then head to bed.

It was several minutes later when he finished the bottle. He took a leak off the deck and then turned to go back inside. The door was locked.

What the fuck, he thought. Did that bitch come behind me and lock the door? He started banging on the door, but no one stirred. Fuck it, he thought as he turned and picked up a chair on the deck. I might as well break the fucking window to get in.

As he was raising the chair up, Angela walked into view.

"Jay, what are you doing?" she screamed. "Put that chair down, now!"

She opened the door as she finished the sentence. Jay was tempted to knock her sideways with the chair, but he decided not to. Instead, he shuffled past her to the bedroom.

CHAPTER 24

Jay was driving around on routine patrol several days later. His souvenir was resting on the top of his duty bag. He had taken Janice's hand and cleaned all of the meat off it. The skeletal hand was just a little too big, so he had cut the little finger off and that was what he had with him.

He thought this would be a good practice from here on out with his victims. He would always try to cut one hand off and then, take the little finger off of that. He still had the rest of Janice's hand back at his house and he would probably always keep the hands hidden away at home, but maybe he would carry the little fingers with him as a good luck charm.

Jay was driving down Lexington Drive when he spotted an unmarked cruiser. He figured it must be one of the detectives. As he passed the maroon car, he saw Dave driving it and he waved to him and then called him on the radio and asked if he could meet him somewhere.

Dave responded in the affirmative. They met up at an empty parking lot where cops routinely went to talk things over.

"Hey buddy. How's it going?" Jay asked.

"Not bad, I guess. These fucking homicide cases are keeping me busy."

"Do you have any new leads on the two teens?"

"Nah, not really. I'm just wondering if any more dead bodies are going to turn up."

"What do you mean? You think there's a serial killer running around out there?" Jay asked him.

"Yes, I do. We have three dead bodies. We also have a missing fourteen-year-old. I don't know who has killed the three victims. I also don't know what's happened to Tony White."

"Damn, Dave. You may be on to something. I hadn't thought about the possibility of a serial killer roaming the streets of Cutler, but maybe there is one here in our midst," Jay said, while fingering Janice's little finger in his hand. The feel of her finger excited him something fierce, but he didn't allow himself to show anything.

"I hope not. The Chief is on me to find the killer of the girl from last fall, and now we have two dead teenagers and other missing people, and I have very few clues to what is happening or who is doing it," Dave lamented.

Jay was ecstatic.

"If there was a serial killer out there, couldn't

you set up some sort of trap for him? What if we had one of the female cops start hanging out in an area where you think he may strike and we could sit back and watch and see what happens. It may be a long shot, but it's something to think about," Jay said.

"You know, you may have an idea. Let me think on it and I'll talk to the Chief about it. I gotta run. Take care, buddy," Dave said as he put his car into gear.

"See ya, Dave."

As Dave drove away, Jay caressed the knuckle of Janice's little finger, silently gloating that he was never going to get caught.

He didn't do much the rest of his shift. He answered one shoplifting call and it was the third offense for the kid. Jay thought about how fucked up that kid was as he was nineteen, yet this was his third offense for petty larceny. In Virginia, the third offense becomes a felony. The boy had stolen about two bucks worth of candy bars, yet he would probably pull some jail time and he would get a felony conviction for it. Hey, better him than me, Jay thought.

* * *

Jay got home that night around 7:30 and when he walked in, his dinner was steaming on the table.

He gave Angela a hug and told her how much he loved her. He kissed her lightly and then went to his bedroom where he removed his uniform, including his gun belt, vest and boots, before returning to eat his dinner.

For once, Angela sat with him and they actually had a good conversation while he ate. She had cooked grilled tuna with green beans and mashed potatoes, one of his favorite dishes. The aroma was magnificent. The taste was even better.

After he finished, Jay asked if they could make love that night, but Angela told him it was that time of the month and she wouldn't be able to.

That rubbed Jay the wrong way, so he got up, got a beer and went out and sat in his recliner. Angela followed him out and told him not to get pissed at her again.

Jay just shrugged and took a gulp of beer, and flipped through the channels trying to find a baseball game to watch. He finally found an Orioles game on the tube, so he kicked back to watch. Angela stormed out of the room.

***

Jay was on his third beer when the kids came tearing up from downstairs and ran through the TV room. Tim tripped and knocked over a plant stand. Jay cursed at him.

"Damn it, Tim. Can't you be more fucking careful?" Jay yelled.

Angela walked into the room at that time. "Jay, calm down, it was an accident."

"Fuck you too, Angela. Can't you control your kids?"

"God damn it, Jay. I'm sick and tired of you

talking to me like this."

This shocked him initially. Then he roared back to life and increased his yelling. Angela, getting more and more frustrated and angry with him by the minute, increased her yelling as well.

Suddenly, Jay smacked Angela on the side of her head, knocking her to the floor. She lay there, crying softly. Jay turned, and Tim and Marie were both peeking around the corner, watching him.

"Get into bed, now, before the both of you get a spanking!" he yelled.

They turned quickly and disappeared from his sight. Jay turned back and saw Angela still lying on the floor. He had mixed feelings about hitting his wife. He had never done anything like this before, but she had been getting out of hand here of late. Maybe this would set her straight.

She sat up, just glaring at Jay, but still crying. She told him she was going to leave with the kids and go to her Mom's house.

Jay told her to pack her shit and get the fuck out of his house if that was what she wanted to do. Crying, Angela got up and went back to the bedroom.

Jay got another beer. About the time he was finishing that one, Angela and the kids walked out, carrying two suitcases. Each kid had a backpack as well. Angela said they were leaving for the night and maybe for good and Jay told her good riddance. He was tired of her shit and he'd be better off if they left.

Angela's eyes glistened as she walked out the front door with the two kids in tow. Both kids were crying as well. They glared at Jay as if he were the devil in disguise.

Fuck her and the two fucking kids, Jay thought. I have Lynn and she loves me. If they don't wanna stay with me, then they can leave. I don't care.

Jay had to work his final daylight shift tomorrow, so he said the next beer would be his last one. As he drained that one fifteen minutes later, his eyes were starting to close. He sat the bottle down and reclined the chair back a little bit more, figuring he'd watch the last inning of the O's game.

He woke up at 4AM to the TV showing static. He dragged himself to the bathroom, took a leak, and then returned to turn the lights and TV off. Then he kicked back in his recliner.

He next awoke to the phone ringing. By the time he got up, the answering machine had kicked on. His Sergeant was talking, asking where he was. Jay picked up the phone, glancing at the clock as he did so. It was 7:30 and he was supposed to be at work at a quarter to 7. He quickly told his Sergeant he had overslept and he would get ready and be into work as soon as he could. The Sergeant told him to hurry his butt up and to get in ASAP.

Hanging up the phone and cursing, Jay kicked it into high gear to shave, shower and get dressed as quickly as he could. By the time he got into work, it was 8:15.

He knew he would probably get written up for this, but he really didn't care. He had a clean record and this was the first time he had ever been late.

When Jay marked 10-41, on duty, his Sergeant

called him and told him to meet him in the municipal parking lot. Jay met him there.

"Why were you late?" His Sergeant asked him.

"I've been going through some shit with Angela. She walked out on me last night and took the kids with her." He omitted the part about hitting and knocking her to the ground.

"I'm going to cut you a break this one time. I'm not going to write you up, but this better not happen again." He then went on cursing the uselessness of women and how they just screwed up everything. Sarge had been married and divorced three times and he was now on his fourth wife.

"Thanks, boss," Jay said just before driving away. He told himself that if Angela was going to get him in trouble at work, maybe he should just slice her throat.

CHAPTER 25

Jay was cruising down Main Street at 11 o'clock that morning when he saw a vehicle heading towards him at breakneck speed. The speed limit was 30 mph on this stretch. His radar started buzzing. He saw in red numbers 54, 55, 56 and it was still increasing. Jay was preparing to do a quick U-turn, when all of a sudden, the car veered into his lane heading right at him.

Jay spun the wheel to the right as quickly as he could. His cruiser was on the shoulder of the road, but the car still hit him squarely on the front, driver side. Jay was doing about 30 mph and he last remembered seeing his radar reading display 63 mph for the other car.

The impact spun him sideways, counterclockwise. The car that was behind him couldn't stop. It hit him on the driver's side, caving his door in on him. His car was then pushed until it broke free and hit a curb. This caused the cruiser to flip over.

Jay was hurt. He was still conscious. He couldn't tell how badly he was hurt. However, he didn't think it was too bad. The air bag had deployed and that had probably saved him. Plus, he was wearing his seat belt as he always did. However, the impact from the second car had crushed the door into him and his shoulder and arm felt fucked up.

He couldn't open his door. It was jammed shut. He was still upside down, but his seatbelt was holding him in. There was some slight smoke in the air. He wasn't sure if this was from the air bag or if the car was on fire. Hell, he wanted out. But, he was stuck.

Jay found his radio mike and called EOC.

"77 to EOC, I was just involved in a 10-50 on Main Street near the high school. I'm upside down. I can't get out of my car. I don't know the condition of the other driver. Get me a supervisor out here and dispatch rescue and fire to the scene."

"10-4, 77, are you okay?"

"My shoulder is a little fuc....excuse me, my arm is hurt, but I'm okay. The car is smoking so get someone here ASAP!"

It seemed like forever before Dave appeared at Jay's car. Though in reality, it may have only been a minute or two. Dave opened his door and helped Jay get out.

"Ow, son of a bitch, that hurts. Careful with my arm."

"Sorry, man. I'll be easy with you."

"Let's get over to the curb. Have a seat. Rescue should be here any second."

"What the fuck happened to that other driver? He was speeding and then came right at me and almost hit me head on. I hope he's charged with reckless driving."

At about that time, rescue pulled up as well as the fire department. The squad went over to the other car, and one of the paramedics from the FD came over to Jay to check him out.

The paramedic, after looking at Jay, told him, "You need to come with us to get your shoulder and arm X-rayed. Something may be broken in there."

"Sure, man," Jay said, grunting from the pain.

Another guy from the ambulance walked over. Jay recognized him.

"Jay, you're a lot luckier than that other fucker."

"Why?"

"He's dead."

"Really? What happened to him?"

Dave walked back at that moment."It looks like the other car spun sideways after hitting you. A dump truck, which was two vehicles behind you, t-boned him. The truck locked his brakes up and slid, pushing the car in front of him, until he came to stop, partially on top of the car. It's messy."

One of the rescue workers chimed in, "He has a strong smell of alcohol about him. He was probably drunk by the way he smells."

Jay thought somehow he must have been attracting death. The world's a fucked up place, but at least I'm a small part in making it a little better.

"Hey, we're ready if you are. Let's go."

"Sure, let's go," Jay said. The pain was really starting to kick in.

One and a half hours later, Jay was finally wheeled into X-Ray. It took another half hour until he got word. Nothing was broken.

However, as the doc told him, he would be sore for several days or weeks, as he'd been hit pretty hard. The doc told him he would give him a prescription for Percocets.

"Thanks, Doc. Am I free to leave now?"

"The nurse still needs to see you. She'll explain about keeping your arm in a sling. She'll also go over how to care for it."

Jay sat back, his arm throbbing, to wait for the nurse. He hoped she would be a young pretty something fresh out of college. However, it was a forty-year-old, sixty-pound overweight nurse with a grumpy attitude.

Well, fuck her too, Jay thought as she finished up and walked away. I never did anything to her; she didn't have to be so pissy with me.

A few minutes later, as Jay was getting ready to get checked out, he saw Angela walk into the room. She came directly over to him and hugged him lightly and kissed him on the cheek.

"Are you okay, Jay?"

"I'm fine. The fucker was drunk and hit me head on. He fucked my arm up, but I came out of it better than he did. He's dead."

They chatted for a few more minutes, but then

Jay asked her if he could borrow her cell phone.

"Why?"

"I want to call Lynn to tell her what happened." Jay said, smiling a little.

"Who is Lynn and why do you need to call her?"

"She's a close friend of mine and well, since you walked out, I was thinking about asking her to move in with me."

Angela stared at Jay for a minute without saying anything. She looked pissed, but she handed him her cell phone. She stood right next to him while he dialed the number.

"Lynn, baby, guess what? I'm in the hospital. Some drunk hit me head on. Yeah, I'm okay, I just fucked my arm up a little bit, but nothing is broke."

He disconnected a few minutes later, after agreeing that Lynn would stop by his house after he got off work.

Angela was just staring at him. Her eyes were narrowed, but he glimpsed a tear in them.

"How old is she, Jay?"

"Twenty-two."

"You are almost old enough to be her father, don't you think?"

"So?"

"Why are you doing this? You've been seeing her for a while, haven't you?"

Jay didn't say anything, but he smiled.

Angela wanted to say something. She opened her mouth, but then closed it. She shook her head and then stormed out of the room.

A few seconds later, Eli and Dave walked in.

They chatted for a bit. Both commented on how pissed Angela seemed when they passed her in the hallway. Jay told them she just didn't understand him.

Eli, once again, told Jay to take as much time as he needed before he came back to work.

"So, what have you heard about the other driver?"

"I've been told he reeked of alcohol. His blood will be tested. Once we know his BAC level and if any drugs were in his system, we'll let you know."

"Who was it?" Jay asked.

"It was one of the local toads, Malcolm Ryan. He was a twenty-three-year old pot head who we've arrested a lot recently."

"Well, well..." Jay said.

"What?" Dave asked.

"I had just gotten the lab results back today for some stuff I took off of him a month and a half ago. It turned out to be meth and I was going to get a felony warrant on him. I guess I don't need to now," Jay said.

"Yeah, you can go ahead and close that case out with an exceptional clearance, suspect died," Eli told Jay.

They chatted for a few more minutes. Then the doctor came back with the written prescription for Jay, telling him that he was cleared to check out of the hospital.

Eli told him he would give him a ride home. Dave told him to take care and that he would see him again soon.

After getting checked out, and after picking up his prescription from the hospital pharmacy, Jay finally made it out to Eli's jeep.

On the ride home, Eli brought up Angela and the situation between her and Jay. Jay told him she was tired of him being a cop and working crazy hours and not spending enough time with her.

Eli, a divorcee himself, told him he knew what he was going through.

"You know, police officers had the highest divorce rate of any profession."

Jay just mumbled something about needing his medication to kick in and then he settled back in the seat.

They traveled the last ten minutes in silence to Jay's house. Once there, Eli told Jay that if he needed anything, to just call him.

"And Jay. Take care of yourself. I was talking with Dave and we are a little worried about you."

"I'm fine, I'm fine. Don't worry." Jay slurred his words slightly. The Percocet was starting to kick in. He just needed to get some rest.

CHAPTER 26

Jay was sitting in his recliner drinking a beer when Lynn got there. His medication was kicking in and the pain had subsided, but he noticed the beer buzz was more intense than usual. Especially, since it seemed he was catching a buzz off the first beer.

She leaned down and gave him a wet kiss on his mouth.

"I wish I could have gotten here earlier, but Al would have really thought it kind of funny if I told him I had to leave early so I could see you," Angela told Jay.

"That's okay, babe. Thanks for coming."

They chatted for a while and then Jay asked her if she could get him another beer.

"Thanks, girl. Do you want to spend the night here tonight? Angela and the kids have moved out.

You're more than welcome to stay the night if you want."

"Jay, I don't know. It's a little early for me to be spending the night with you."

"Hell, girl, just stay and be my nurse for the night. Don't worry, I'm too tired and this medication is screwing with me. I'll probably pass out after another beer or two anyways."

"Ok, I'll stay here. What do you want for dinner?"

"I don't know. I'm really not that hungry. Feel free to look around the kitchen to see what we have. Help yourself to anything in the house."

Lynn went into the kitchen and Jay could hear her opening and closing the cupboard doors. Finally, she returned.

"I couldn't find much at all. There was a frozen pizza in the freezer, so I stuck that in the oven."

Jay had one more beer while waiting on the pizza and then another one with the pizza. By the time he was finished eating, he was feeling pretty good. Damn, he thought, these pills are good shit, especially with beer.

"Are you okay? You look a little funny."

"I'm feeling great." Jay stood up, staggered a little, and then walked over to her and gave her a big hug and a kiss.

The kissing intensified and Jay asked Lynn if they could go into the bedroom.

"Go on in and get ready. I'm going to clean up a bit and then be right there." Lynn put the dirty dishes in the dishwasher and got it going and then she wiped down the counter and the table. Ten minutes after Jay had left, she finished up and walked back to his bedroom.

"Jay?"

Jay didn't answer. He was lying nude in the bed, but he was snoring away. She pulled the sheet and a blanket up over him and he never stirred.

Jay woke up at 10AM the next morning to find Lynn was gone. He didn't even find a note from her. After he had two cups of coffee and a bowl of oatmeal, he tried to call her, but just got her voice mail. He hung up without leaving a message.

His head was pounding. He felt as if his entire body had gotten run over by a truck. His arm was throbbing, so he took two more pills. He thought about drinking a beer, but decided against it.

Jay didn't do much that day. He watched TV and dozed off several times. He tried calling Lynn again in the afternoon, but he didn't get her.

* * *

That evening, Angela came back. She walked into the house while Jay was eating some macaroni and cheese. She was alone.

"The kids are at my mother's house. I want to talk."

They sat and talked for a good forty-five minutes. Jay never apologized, but he did tell Angela he would like for her to come back. He didn't know the story with Lynn and even though she was a great fuck, maybe she wasn't the type to settle down with him, so maybe he should hold onto Angela for a little while longer.

"If I do move back in, you need to change a few things."

Number one, he had to cut back on his drinking. She said she wouldn't tolerate him getting drunk almost every night of the week. Number two, his attitude towards both her and the kids better change immediately and the cussing better stop as well. Number three, if he as much as raised a hand at her again, she would be gone and would take him for everything she could. Number four, he better stop fucking around with other girls.

Jay thought for a few minutes and then agreed to all of the conditions. Angela said the kids were going to stay at her mother's house that night, but she would bring them back home tomorrow after she got off of work.

Jay said that would be fine. They sat around talking for another hour or so and then Jay said he was going to bed. He said the pain medicine was making him drowsy. He might as well get to bed early, and hopefully by tomorrow he would feel better.

Angela told him she would be up for several more hours and that she would be leaving early in the morning to go to work. She walked him to the bedroom. She gave him a hug, holding onto him a little longer than normal. She kissed him lightly on his lips and told him maybe in a day or two, they could make love again.

"Hey, that sounds great. I want to do it with you

tonight, but I'm afraid I'll fall asleep on you."

"That's okay, honey. Get your rest."

"I'll call you in the morning after I get up. I'll probably still be sleeping when you leave."

Angela said good night, kissed him again and walked out, shutting the bedroom door behind her.

The next few days went by with no major problems or drinking episodes. Each day, he felt a little better and by the fourth day, he was ready to take the sling off his arm. It still wasn't one hundred percent, but it was a lot better than it had been just a few days ago. He figured after two or three more days, he'd be ready to go back to work.

When Jay's kids came back home, he took them aside one at a time and had a good talk with each of them. He explained he'd been going through some rough times, but he loved both of them very much and he was sorry for how he'd been treating them. Neither child said a lot, but they both gave him a hug when he asked for one.

CHAPTER 27

Dave knew he had a serial killer on his hands. Was it a cop? He wasn't sure. If it was, which one was it? It could be Jay, but then again, it might not be.

There was another missing person. This time, it was a nineteen-year-old college student. Her name was Janice Thompson. She was from upstate New York, some small mountain town. Her folks had been down once and talked with him. If it hadn't been for the three murdered people and Tony White being missing, he might have thought she had just run off.

However, he was now wondering if Tony and Janice's bodies might turn up. He was treating both cases as possible homicides, even though he didn't have any evidence pointing toward this.

There was one clue though, that alone, would mean very little. Two days before Janice was reported missing, Jay had marked off with her. He had given Janice a courtesy ride back to her apartment. Jay had marked off with her when he arrived, but had only stayed there for three minutes.

Jay, as much as he hated to admit it, was a suspect. He really thought that he would eventually rule Jay out as a suspect. But, for the time being, he couldn't. Jay had been working during the time period the first girl was killed last fall. He also had been working the night the teens turned up missing.

Any of those clues alone, would mean absolutely nothing. And, even together, they may not mean a thing. However, another wrench thrown into the equation was Jay had now killed two people in the line of duty.

Dave had gone over all of this many times in his mind. He had not talked to any other person about it, yet.

Dave had been doing a little snooping. Jay was having marital problems. Now, once again, that didn't mean a lot. The divorce rate in the police profession was very high. Police work typically had a high stress level. A cop who kills in the line of duty would have his stress level ratcheted up another notch. All of that could lead to either a stronger marriage, or it could put a strain on a marriage.

In Jay's case, it has appeared to break up his marriage, at least for the time being. Dave also suspected that Jay was getting himself involved with the inspector upstairs, Lynn. He hadn't actually seen the two of them together. But, he had heard the rumors.

Besides these coincidences, he had no real evidence that pointed to Jay as the suspect. He'd known Jay for years now. They were buddies. There was no way that he could be a cold-blooded killer.

Dave had talked to Jay several times since he first made him a suspect. Jay had seemed perfectly normal to him. He hadn't said anything that led Dave to believe that he was the killer. Yet, he didn't say anything that relieved him of being a suspect.

Dave told himself that he would keep plugging away. He sure as hell hoped that he could rule Jay out. One day, he hoped, the two of them could have a beer together and Dave might even tell him about the suspicions he'd had. They both could laugh about it. Until that time though, he had to treat Jay as a suspect.

* * *

Lynn realized she had fallen in love with a married man. The last thing she wanted to do was to break up a marriage. She kept telling herself their marriage was already on the rocks and she wasn't the cause of it.

Jay was a fascinating person. He was quite a bit older than she was. He was good looking and she liked being around him. He had been through a lot, especially in the past few months. She thought he handled it all fairly well.

She thought back to the other night. Against her better judgment, she had told Jay she would spend the night. He needed someone to watch over him. He had passed out early on. That gave her the opportunity to walk around his house.

She could easily see he was a family man. There were pictures all over the house of his kids in various stages of growing up. She also saw that he had several guns around the house. They were locked up. She knew Jay was a cop, but guns still scared her. He also had two knives lying on top of his dresser.

They were the type of knives that cops carried in their pockets. She had seen one in Jay's pocket several times.

She also saw his gun belt lying on his dresser. She assumed the pistol in the holster was the one that had killed two people. She didn't know how he could have killed two people and not have it affect him.

She had settled down on the bed next to Jay a little after midnight. Jay had still been sleeping soundly. She needed to get some sleep as well. Just as she was dozing off, she heard her cell phone ringing. By the time she got out of bed, it had stopped ringing.

She saw the number and immediately called it back. What she was told shook her up badly. She left the house without waking Jay or even leaving him a note.

CHAPTER 28

It had been two months since Jay's car accident and he was getting back to being his old self. His old, crazy self, that is. He was just about ready to kill his ninth victim. Well, to be exact, it was his seventh, as two were killed in the line of duty. He really couldn't count them.

She was a young twenty-something whom he had found walking alone at 2AM. He was going to give her a courtesy ride home. They never made it.

She was half drunk and high to boot. Jay moved his duty bag and told her to sit in the front seat, as it was more comfortable than the back seat of his cruiser. She readily agreed to sit up front.

Jay had Janice's little finger stuck in his drink holder and he caressed it as the girl got into his car. It was late at night and they were in a dark section of town, so he really doubted that anyone saw her get in. He didn't log anything with EOC.

He wondered if he could fuck this girl prior to killing her and he figured he would try. Shit, he would do it while on duty and that would be another first for him.

Jay decided to drive back to the park and went down the same trail where he'd found the two teens. He drove all the way down the trail until he reached the beginning of the old logging road.

The girl was quite friendly and talkative. Jay knew he wouldn't have any trouble with her. He was right. When they pulled onto the trail, she'd asked him where they were going and Jay told her he wanted a little privacy with her. She smiled and said okay.

Once he got backed in between a group of trees, he shut the car off, leaving the radio tuned to a local pop station. He asked if he could kiss her and she said sure, why not.

She was a fun, bubbly type of girl who seemed to be willing to try anything. Jay wasn't sure what she was on, but he knew she was on something. She wasn't the most attractive girl, but at 2AM on a slow night, did it really matter?

The kissing progressed to Jay taking her shirt off and then Jay asked her if she wanted to climb in the back seat. The girl told him she'd never made love in the back seat of a car, much less a police car, but sure, why not?

Jay fucked her hard and she gave it right back to him. It was wild and they were both drenched in

Twisted Obsession

sweat by the time they were done. It was mid-July and it was very humid.

Jay climbed out of the back seat, panting a bit. The girl followed him.

"That was great. Did you ever think you'd fuck a cop in the back seat of his car?"

"No, but I'm glad I did."

They stood there, nude and cooled back down a bit. After a few minutes, they both slowly began to get dressed. While dressing, Jay told the girl he was going to show her a wild cave that had some crazy looking rocks in it. She was game, so, wearing just his pants and boots, he drove down the logging road until he came to the cave where the teens had been killed.

The bodies of the teens had been found several months ago, late in the month of May. Jay figured Dave was finished collecting evidence from the cave so he had no reason to come back out to it.

Jay got out and grabbed his flashlight. He felt to make sure his knife was still in his pocket. It was. He shined his light and showed the girl the entrance to the cave.

Jay walked her into the cave, shining his light around.

"Hey, the coolest looking rocks are near the back of the cave."

Jay walked her well past the spot where he had killed the teens, just to be on the safe side. This cave went on and on as many of the caves did in this area and Jay walked with her for a long way.

When he felt they were far enough in, he went

to the girl and took her in an embrace and started kissing her. She reacted by kissing him back. He thought about fucking her again and figured if he could, he would.

He could and he did. He found a spot where the rock was flat, with no jagged corners sticking up. She was really into making love with him. He made sure he stayed on top. He didn't want to screw his back up on the rock.

It was just as much fun as the first time and when he was all done, he took his knife and sliced the bitch a new airway in her throat. The look in her eyes as his knife was doing its deed was priceless. He wished he could catch some of these looks in a picture, but he never remembered to have a camera with him. Maybe next time, he thought.

She didn't die right away, but unlike some of the others, he didn't stab her anymore. She was bleeding freely and it wouldn't take long for her to die. She grunted and gasped. She was in obvious pain. She rolled around and tried to get up several times, but couldn't. It was only a minute or two until she went unconscious.

Once she passed on, Jay thought about covering her in rocks, but he was already tired and didn't feel like it. Also, he didn't have his hatchet and he didn't think his knife would be too good at cutting through bone. Hell, though, he might as well try, so he took the serrated edge and started sawing on her little finger, just below the knuckle. The finger came off with surprising ease.

Ah ha, another souvenir, he thought. Just then,

he realized that he was in this cave without his radio and if anyone had been trying to call him, he would be in trouble. He felt himself break into a cold sweat. Shit, he had to stop killing people on the spur of the moment.

Jay made his way out of the cave and back to his cruiser as quickly as he could. It was 3:30 and the radio was quiet. Had anyone tried to call him and were they now looking for him? He didn't know, but he figured he'd wait to see what the next radio traffic was.

In the meanwhile, he found an old rag in his trunk and he used that to wipe some sweat and blood off his body. He then got himself dressed back in uniform. He had the AC cranked up and once dressed, with his vest and gun belt back on, he sat in front of the full blast of the cold air until he cooled down some.

Once cooled down, Jay drove down the logging roads, to the trail and finally to the park. No one was in the park and in another minute, he was out onto a city street. Still, there was no sound from his radio.

Jay decided to do something to make sure that no one was out looking for him. Within a few blocks from the park, he saw a vehicle heading towards him with one headlight out. As the vehicle passed, Jay got a partial tag but couldn't make out the entire thing, only that it was a VA tag and had started with the letters WWS.

The car was an older Mustang, dark blue or black in color. Jay made a quick U-turn and then sped up to the car and activated his lights. Normally, within a few seconds, a car would start slowing. However, this car immediately sped up. Jay was able to read the entire tag now, WWSS-5467, and called in that he was attempting a traffic stop on S. Magnolia Avenue, but the car seemed to be running. He gave the tag. In a moment, it came back to a Ford Contour and the tag was reported as being stolen.

Shit, that meant maybe the car was stolen as well. Jay was now going about 55 mph through a residential neighborhood. He turned his siren on as well as his lights. When the car got to Main Street, it turned left and then nailed it. Jay called in his direction of travel and pushed his gas petal to the floor. His radar unit told him he was going 85 mph and the Mustang was still pulling away ever so slowly.

Hell, pursuits always got his blood pumping. He called his Sergeant and told him the speed and where they were heading. He repeated the tags were stolen and the car may be as well. The Sergeant told him to do his best to stick with it. The county and state police were being notified in case the suspect made it out of the city.

The Mustang turned westbound on Mt. Carmel Road and slid sideways as it did so. A cloud of smoke was around the car. It barely pulled itself out of the slide just prior to the edge of the road. The driver punched it again.

Mt. Carmel had some long straight sections on it. Jay thought maybe he could catch up to the Mustang on one of these long stretches. The Mustang was quicker, but he thought his Crown Victoria probably had more top-end speed.

He proved himself right while on one long stretch. His foot had the gas pedal pressed completely to the floorboards. His radar read 110. He felt his knuckles clenched to the steering wheel. He consciously told himself to relax. He was starting to zone. He had to stay focused. He was gaining on the Mustang.

Jay had kept everyone advised as to his location. A county unit advised he was at the city limits on Mt. Carmel Road, getting ready to deploy the stop sticks.

They were about a half-mile from the city limits. Jay was less than twenty feet from the rear of the Mustang. The county unit had advised his exact location. His cruiser was hidden. Jay knew the stop sticks would flatten the tires of the Mustang. They were always thrown from the right hand side of the road.

Jay thought fast. There was no oncoming traffic. He knew he had to be close to the spot, so he got into the opposite lane of travel and backed it off just a bit. He did not want to hit those strips and flatten his own tires.

He saw it when it happened. The Mustang hopped just a tad and slowed down. It kept going, but steadily got slower and slower. Jay could see rubber tearing off the tires. Finally, one rear tire came completely off. Now the car was riding on its rim. Red sparks were flying and the car had slowed down a lot, but it was still running hard.

By this time, there were two other cruisers behind him. Jay was focused. He was not going to let this fucker get away. Suddenly, the Mustang slammed on its brakes and pulled over near a closed Chevron Station. Both doors opened and two black males jumped out and started running. Jay was out in a heartbeat as were the other two officers.

The foot pursuit lasted a minute, if that long. All of the officers were in better shape then these two toads. Jay tackled one and Ben tackled the other. Cuffs were slapped on in seconds and as quick as that, it was over.

Jay was panting hard and sweat was rolling off him. He was pumped and if this guy gave him any shit, he was going to slam him.

Jay asked the driver why he didn't stop. The answer almost made him laugh.

"I ain't got no license, man."

"Dude, you would've gotten a simple ticket for driving with no OL. Now, you are facing charges of eluding, reckless driving and more. Stupid. Oh, and I know the tags on your car are stolen, and probably your car too. You're going to jail for a long time, Bud."

The young male didn't say anything as Jay walked him to his cruiser. He was thinking how lucky he was. Now if anyone saw he was sweaty or just worn out, they would think it was from the chase. His luck was getting better and better.

God, I'm fucking invincible, Jay thought.

CHAPTER 29

"Are you sure you're okay, Jay? You really seemed to be a lot more stressed lately," Eli said with a look of concern in his eyes.

"I'm fine, why?"

"Jay, over the past year, you've had more happen to you than most folks have in a lifetime. You've shot and killed two people. You were hit head on by a drunk driver who died and you got hurt from that. And now, just a few nights ago, you got in a car chase and foot pursuit."

"So what? A lot has happened, but that doesn't mean I'm stressed or anything."

"Besides all of that, you and Angela separated briefly. I'm also hearing through the grapevine that you and that hot chick up in Inspections may be having a fling."

"Eli," Jay said laughing, "Angela and I may have had some problems, but everything is working itself out. As far as Lynn goes, we've become good friends, but nothing else has happened, not even a simple kiss. Hell, lord knows I'd love to kiss her and do a lot more, but we haven't."

"Okay, I just want to make sure that you're all right before you leave for your break. If you need me for anything or just want to talk, don't hesitate to call. I'll be honest with you Jay, I am concerned about you. But I know you have it in you to pull through all of this okay and to come back better than before," Eli told him.

"I'm fine, boss. Don't worry about me. Tell you what, though, I'll try to give you a call sometime during the next week just to relieve your mind, you old worry wart."

Eli laughed at that and clapped Jay on the back as he was walking out of the office.

* * *

Jay was on his last daylight prior to his seven-day break and he was looking forward to getting some time off. He hadn't seen too much of Lynn the past few weeks, but he planned to see a lot more of her over the next week.

His relationship with Lynn was getting better and better. The other month when he had passed out on her and awakened to find her gone had got him thinking that maybe it wasn't going to work out between them.

However, Lynn explained to him several days later that her best friend from college had been killed in a car accident. She'd freaked and left all of a sudden to go back to her hometown for the funeral. She'd apologized profusely, but Jay told her not to worry about it.

Lynn was young and was not used to having friends or family die, so she was bound to take it hard.

Jay had two more hours of his shift left and then he would get his seven days off. Shift work really wore on him at times, but the seven-day break once a month helped to make it worthwhile. Especially now that he knew he'd probably get a chance to see Lynn several times during the week.

Jay also thought of something else he was planning. He was going to go to Richmond sometime during the week to see if he could find a suitable tenth victim. Jay smiled evilly again as he reached over to his duty bag and caressed Janice's little finger.

At 6:30, a two-officer call came out for a domestic in progress. It was physical. The female said her boyfriend had a knife. Once again, just like that domestic call from last year, Jay was only a few blocks away.

Jay rounded the corner. He came to stop one house away from the actual address. He could see two figures inside the house through a large picture window.

"EOC, I'm on location," Jay radioed. "It appears that there are two people fighting inside the residence. I'm moving in closer to get a better look."

Ben called and said he'd be there in about thirty seconds and to keep him appraised of the situation.

Jay crept up to the side of the white, vinyl-sided house. He remembered the dispatcher had told him a knife was involved. The safe zone when someone had a knife is twenty-one feet.

He heard a female screaming bloody murder and he heard a guy yelling back at her. He couldn't make out the words they were saying. They were yelling a lot, though. As he was about to bang on the door and announce his presence, he heard the female yelling again.

"For God's sake, put the knife down," he heard a female voice say.

Her yelling changed to frantic screaming.

At that time, Jay kicked the door in and ran inside, gun drawn, yelling, "Police Department, drop the knife!"

The male, a scraggly-looking white guy with long, dark hair turned and held the knife up. He yelled, "Get the fuck away from me."

Jay yelled again, "Drop the knife. Drop the knife and nobody will get hurt."

He could see the girl behind the guy. She was still screaming and her face was bloodied up, but Jay was not hearing her at all. Jay was only about ten feet away from the guy.

Shit, I'm too close, but I can't back out with this girl still being in here.

"Drop the knife, man and nobody's going to get hurt. Drop it now!" Jay yelled.

"Fuck you, pig, get the fuck out of my house before I kill the both of you."

Jay imagined the guy was wired on some kind of drug, but he didn't know what. Meth, more than likely. That caused people to do some crazy things. He got a look at the girl. She was wired on something as well by the look in her eyes.

Jay told him he wasn't leaving. At that time, he heard a noise behind him. He turned his head ever so slightly to take a peek. It was Ben entering the house with his gun drawn. When the guy saw the second cop with his gun out, he turned and before they could react, he grabbed the girl and held the knife to her throat. He said he was going to slice the bitch right now if they didn't get outta his house.

Ben and Jay were about three feet apart. Both had their guns drawn. Both were yelling, "Drop the knife, drop the knife."

All of a sudden, the girl elbowed the guy in the groin area. He doubled over in pain, dropping the knife. She bolted out of the room.

Jay jumped first and tackled the guy, who started fighting like a wildcat. His gun was back in his holster with the security snap snapped down on it holding the .40 caliber Glock in place.

The guy's elbow caught Jay on his nose. Damn, that hurt. I think that fucker just broke my nose so fuck him he's dead. Jay got the guy in a chokehold with his right arm and then reached around and pulled his asp out with his left. He didn't snap it open. He kept it closed. He started ramming it as hard as he could into the rib and kidney area of this crazy guy.

Ben eventually pulled him off the guy and slapped a pair of cuffs on him. Jay was fired up and was ready to kill the guy.

The crazy guy was still breathing, but there was blood trickling out of his mouth.

As both cops were catching their breath, Jay heard sirens in the distance. Ben radioed to the other units that they had the suspect in custody and everyone was 10-4.

At about this time, the girl came out of nowhere and hit Ben on the side of the head with a ceramic plant vase, dropping him in an instant. Jay pulled out his pepper spray and sprayed the girl. Whatever she was on had her so wired, the pepper spray had no effect. She bent over and picked up the knife.

She screamed, "No one beats my boyfriend like that and gets away with it!"

She lunged towards Jay and he shot her twice, point blank, center mass, dropping her quicker than Ben had fallen. Those hydro-shock bullets really worked well, he thought. She looked like she was dead before she ever hit the floor.

Jay checked on Ben. He was still unconscious. He was breathing well and had a strong pulse. Then he got on his radio.

* * *

"EOC, EOC and all units responding. My partner is down, get me rescue ASAP. Also, one suspect is down and you better call the Medical Examiner."

Twisted Obsession

Within a few seconds, more officers were arriving on scene. The Sergeant, after surveying the scene, put out his hand and asked for Jay's gun.

Jay handed it to him without a word. The Sergeant in turn handed him his gun.

"It's standard procedure, Jay," said the Sergeant.

"I know, shit, this is the third time this has happened to me. I'm getting used to it."

Jay was standing outside. He was literally drained, both mentally and physically. His legs were quivering and his hand was trembling. Blood was crusting in his nostrils. An officer walked by, smoking a cigarette.

"Hey buddy, can I get one of those from you?"

"Thanks."

He stood there smoking his first cigarette in fifteen years when Dave pulled up. He walked up and immediately put his arm around Jay and asked him if he was okay.

"Life works in strange ways, man. No cop here has killed anyone in the line of duty in thirty years. Now you've done it three times in less than a year."

"I know. It's weird, but when I saw Ben falling and that girl turned towards me with a knife in her hand, I never thought twice about pulling the trigger. Stupid bitch, I'm glad she's dead, but I hope Ben is going to be okay."

"I'll check on him. I'll come back out and let you know. Hey, when did you take up smoking?"

"Just now, buddy. Don't worry, I'll have one or two, but that'll be it for me."

CHAPTER 30

Once again, Jay was home with several days off. The Department was going to take a close look at him now after killing a third person during the line of duty. However, this one, just like the others, was completely justified. But, he had killed three people in a year's time. What would they do with him?

The media was really eating this one up. The headline read, "Jay Mundie, a decorated veteran of sixteen years, shot and killed a nineteen-year-old mother of one today." Just underneath, in only slightly smaller print, it said, "This was the third person that Mundie had killed in the line of duty in the past ten months."

Jay was on his fourth beer of the night. Tonight he was drinking Williamsburg Stock Ale and it said right on the label that both George Washington and

Patrick Henry used to drink this brand.

Hey, if it's good enough for the first President of the United States, then it's good enough for me.

I've been sitting here just wasting time, thought Jay. Damn, what am I going to do?

Jay shook his head. What was happening to him? He thoroughly enjoyed killing people. That wasn't a problem, but he knew both his drinking and his drug use were increasing.

As long as I stay away from needles and snorting and smoking shit like crack and meth, I should be okay.

Angela was at work and the kids were in school. Jay didn't normally drink during the day, but he was today. Hell, he might as well call Lynn at work and see what she was doing.

She answered on the third ring. Jay could tell she was happy to hear from him.

"Hey girl. I want to see you today."

"Have you been drinking already?"

"I've had a few, but I'll stop if that's a problem."

"I can probably slip out by three. Can you meet me at my place?"

"Call me as soon as you walk out the door. I'll leave as soon as I hear from you and I'll be waiting for you at your house."

"Please don't drink any more beer between now and then, okay?"

Jay agreed.

* * *

He was waiting when she got there. She pulled up, smiling, walked up to him and gave him a hug.

"Come on baby, what's wrong?"

"I'm just worried the Department is going to do something to me. All three killings were justified and they damn well know it, but the media is playing it up. The Department might find some excuse to let me go if they think their own asses are on the line."

"Jay. You don't really believe that, do you?"

"I don't know. I'm getting to where I don't trust anyone anymore, just you and Angela."

"Jay, I'm not going to keep doing this forever. Either you leave her and we get together, or we should just stop seeing each other."

"Baby, come on now. We have something good going, why do you want to screw it up?"

The phone rang before she could answer. When Lynn picked up, she called Jay and told him it was for him.

"Who is it? No one knows I'm here."

"It sounds like Angela."

It was Angela. She spoke loudly and incoherently at first, but he soon got her to settle down. She told him a car had hit Tim while he was riding his bike. He was hurt pretty bad. She didn't think he was wearing his helmet.

"How is he?"

"They flew him to UVA. My God, Jay, what if he dies? I'm so scared," she cried to him.

"What was he doing riding his bike when he's supposed to be in school?"

"The principal thinks he skipped out early. What

the fuck, Jay, Tim is hurt badly and you're worried about him skipping school? Jay, I'm heading out now to go to UVA. Do you want to meet me there or should I pick you up?"

"Can you pick me up? I've had a little bit to drink."

"Shit Jay, what's happening to you? Goddamn, my son is in a bike accident and his fucking father is drunk and with his girlfriend. Yeah, right, I'll be there in fifteen minutes."

As Jay hung up, he wondered how Angela knew he was at Lynn's and where she lived.

Jay met Angela outside when she arrived about fifteen minutes later. She was shaken up, but all in all, she seemed to be holding it together pretty well. She told him that Marie was at her parents' house.

The ride to UVA was fairly quiet. Jay was scared that Tim would be messed up for life and he hoped and prayed he wouldn't be.

When they got there and finally found a place to park, Jay and Angela rushed into the hospital. They ran up to the ER desk. A nurse stopped them. Angela was crying, so Jay asked where they could find Tim. They were fortunate as the door they used to enter took them to the correct wing.

Once they were pointed in the correct direction, they quickly found where Tim was. He was in for X-rays. A nurse told them to have a seat as he should be done fairly soon.

They had just sat down when a doctor came walking up. He introduced himself as Dr. Tolliver. Jay thought he looked awfully strange to be a doctor, as he didn't appear to have a hair on his head, not even eyebrows or eyelashes.

The doc told them that nothing appeared broken, but he might have a slight concussion. He needed to spend the night in the hospital to make sure he was going to be fine.

Both Angela and Jay were relieved to hear that Tim was going to be okay. The doc showed them to the room where Tim was. He was obviously banged up, but more than that, he was sleepy, probably due to the medication they had given him.

After the doc left, they chatted for a few more minutes. Tim's eyes were drooping and he was continually yawning. Jay was worried that if he had a head injury, maybe he should be kept awake. However, a nurse told him if was fine and best if Tim could go to sleep. So, they said their goodbyes and Jay and Angela left. They were both still shaken up. However, it was a relief to have talked to Tim. No matter if he was bruised and sore, his brain was not injured. That was the best news of all.

It was in the car that Angela brought up Lynn.

"What's the deal with you two? I thought you were going to stop seeing her."

"Angela, she's just a close friend and we have a lot in common."

"Bullshit, Jay. You two are a lot more than friends and you know it. I'm not blind and I'm not stupid."

Jay didn't know what to say, so he just kept his mouth shut.

"Jay, I've been thinking a lot about us and I've

made a decision. If you want to keep screwing Lynn, just stop being so fucking obvious about it."

Jay was stunned. What was his wife telling him?

"Angie, baby, it's not really like that."

"Jay, cut the shit and be honest with me for once. I know what you're doing. Let's just say I've got pictures. You want to keep denying everything now?"

Jay started to stammer something, but stopped when Angela cut him off.

"Just stay quiet for a minute and let me say my piece. If you want to screw some hot twenty-something, then that's your decision.

"Hey, I've been telling you . . ."

Jay stopped when he saw her look.

"Jay, I'm in my late thirties and we have two young children. If I leave you, our lives will get worse. If you can just cut down on your drinking and stop treating us so fucking bad, then do what you must with Lynn. Just keep it quiet and don't flaunt it and don't let the children ever find out about this."

Jay was shocked. Hell, miracles never cease, do they?

As they pulled in the driveway, Angela told Jay that she still loved him.

"Please, just keep everything quiet. Don't bring her to our house and stop the fucking excessive drinking and cussing and life will be just fine."

Jay agreed, thinking how he must be the luckiest man in the word.

CHAPTER 31

Dave felt he was getting closer to solving the homicides. He wasn't sure why he thought this, but he did. He kept going over the few clues he had in his mind. Thinking constantly on this was enough to drive him mad. However, he kept dwelling on the murders.

He had a gut feeling Jay was somehow involved with the killings. How, he did not know. A year ago, if someone had suggested to him that Jay, his buddy, would kill a person in cold blood, he would have laughed at them. Now, he wasn't so sure.

He hated to feel this way. He really hoped that a clue would turn up that would prove Jay was innocent. Something just kept gnawing at the back of him mind. He couldn't put his finger on what it was.

He had been watching Jay. Well, as much as one cop can watch another one without him seeing you, he thought. He had proven, to himself at least, that Jay was involved with Lynn, the girl in Inspections. Dave laughed at that. Lynn was one hot girl. If he had the opportunity, he would have asked her out himself.

Dave knew Jay liked to go up in the mountains. The two of them used to go hiking a lot of years ago, before wives and kids came along. Wow, the last time we went up there together must have been ten years ago. Where does time go?

Dave knew Jay used to spend a lot of time in the mountains. He knew the trails inside and out. There were literally hundreds of miles of trails up there. Some trails were hiked on a daily basis. A few were hiked maybe once a year.

If someone decided to dispose of a body on a remote mountain trail, the odds could be against it being discovered. Of course, if this was the case, some unsuspecting hiker might discover a body tomorrow.

Unless this was to happen, he would have to go with the clues he had. Which were darn few. Jay was a suspect in his mind mainly due to a strong gut feeling. He couldn't explain his gut feeling. And he couldn't get a warrant based on his feelings.

Dave would stick with it, though. If it took six days or six years, he would stick on this case until he solved it. He was confident that something would turn up. Some clue, some shred of evidence or some witness. Something would happen that would help him to break this case wide open.

Until something did happen, Dave hoped and prayed no more murders would take place. There had been too many killings already. Plus, he thought there was a good chance that at least one of the missing persons would eventually turn up to be dead.

Dave also was shocked that Jay had killed another person in the line of duty. It was justified. But damn, three line of duty killings by the same officer in less than a year. It was unheard of for an officer to kill someone in the line of duty in Cutler, much less to kill three.

Dave had gone over each killing. No matter how he looked at them, Jay had done the correct thing in each case. Dave had spoken with many witnesses to all of the killings. They all said the same thing. Jay didn't have a choice in what he did.

What would killing three people in the line of duty do to a cop? Killing someone was what each and every officer prayed would never happen to them. But, officers had to mentally prepare themselves in case this day ever came. It had come for Jay three times.

Dave was going over all of this in his mind when his phone rang. It was the shift commander on duty.

"Detective, we think we found one of your missing persons."

"Which one?"

"We think it's the juvenile, Tony White."

"Is he dead?"

"Yes, a fisherman hooked him in the quarry. He wasn't sure what he had snagged. He told us his curiosity was raised because he had fished there for years without ever getting caught on even a tree limb.

"So, did he get the body out of the water?"

"No. His son was with him. His son swims on the high school swim team and is also one of the team's top divers. So, he had his son dive into the water to see if he could find what had snagged his line. His son came back up pretty quick after finding the kid."

"Have you called the dive team in?"

"Yes, I called them just before I called you."

"Ok, I'll be there in 20 minutes. Just keep the scene secured until I get there."

Damn, Dave thought. Here's one more body that has turned up. I have to figure this out.

He couldn't be sure this juvenile's death could be tied in with the others. Odds are it could, though. The kid had been missing for months now. If he had been under water for that long, there might not be a lot left of him.

The first thing they had to do was to get the body out of the water. Then, it would have to get sent to the lab. An autopsy would be done to determine the cause of death. Hopefully, the autopsy would provide a clue he could use to solve the case. If not, it would just get more frustrating for him.

Frustration would fuel Dave to work all the harder. He had learned that about himself on previous cases. The harder a case was, the more he got frustrated with it, the more he stuck with it. He was known for his ability to solve the tough ones. The string of homicides he was currently working were his toughest cases yet. He told himself that the end result of these cases would be just like his other cases. He would solve them, arrest the suspect and take the case to court.

CHAPTER 32

Jay wiped the sweat off his brow as he took a drink of water from his canteen. Damn, it sure is hot today, even up in the mountains. Jay had decided to head up to Skyline Drive and to do a little hiking. He used to hike quite a bit, but in recent years, he'd gotten so busy between the job and family, he'd gotten away from it. He figured it was as good a time as any to start back.

He estimated he'd hiked about four miles or so. It was a little after 2PM and he was starting to get hungry. He'd started off on the Smith's Run Trail at milepost 74. He'd left his truck parked at the Smith's Run Parking area and his intent was to hike out, turn around and come back.

Jay had made it to Smith's Run Falls at about 11AM. It was his first time there and he found it to be a beautiful spot. The waterfalls were forty-two feet tall, according to the small map that he'd picked up at the Ranger Station. It was so peaceful watching the water flow across the rocks as it made its downward travels down the falls and into the creek at the bottom.

He'd rested at the falls for twenty minutes or so before starting up again. His original thoughts were to turn around at Smith's Run Falls, but he decided to keep on going once he'd rested.

According to his map, Oak Tree Falls was not too far away. He guessed it to be about a mile and a half. He'd made good time, making it to Oak Tree Falls in about forty minutes. There were actually two sets of waterfalls here, one twenty-eight feet high and the other sixty-three feet high. These were even more beautiful than Smith's Run Falls.

He had eaten a granola bar while at Oak Tree Falls and had some water, but that had been it so far. Jay had walked past McCoy's Gap Fire Road about a hundred yards back. Looking at his map, he figured he had to be getting close to the Oak Tree River Cabin.

He found a small clearing and decided to stop, rest and eat a bit. Jay took off his small backpack and took out his lunch. He had a pack of tuna fish with some crackers, so he made some mini-tuna fish sandwiches. Jay also had a banana, two apples and some grapes. He ate the banana, grapes and one of the apples. He also emptied his canteen of water, but he was carrying another jug of water in his backpack.

After eating, Jay lay down and put his head on his pack and thought for a while. He'd not seen another person since he had left Smith's Run Falls. It was peaceful and tranquil here. He wished it could always be like this.

Well, damn, it probably is always like this, I'm just not here all the time to experience it, he thought. Jay was watching a squirrel hop from branch to branch when he felt himself start to drift off. He allowed himself to fall asleep, as he knew he would probably wake up in ten or fifteen minutes.

Instead, he slept for thirty minutes, waking to hear a branch snap near him. He sat up, reaching for his Glock while he cleared his head. There, not ten feet away from him, was a deer. It was an average-sized doe and it was not frightened at all when he moved.

Jay held his hand out to the animal, and ever so slowly it started walking towards him. But as much as he coaxed it, the deer would not come closer than four feet to him. He thought about getting the apple out of his pack, but he didn't.

As he was watching this one, another doe stepped out onto the path and came toward him as well. This is pretty wild, he thought. Here I am out in the mountains, and a couple of wild deer are acting like they are tame and walking right up to me. Shit, people have really messed this park up when the wild animals have become tame.

However, he still loved watching them. They stayed nearby for several minutes, but they finally wandered away, back into the trees, when they realized he wasn't going to feed them.

Jay sat there for several more minutes, sipping his water, and then he finally got up and started walking again.

After about fifteen minutes, a cabin came into sight. This must be the Oak Tree River Cabin, Jay thought. It was gray and looked old. As he got closer, he saw a towel hanging off the front porch.

The cabin was small. The logs were dark and weathered. From where he stood, the cabin appeared to only be big enough to have two rooms. The area in front of the porch was dirt. The other sides of the cabin had brush growing up to within a few feet of the walls.

Jay decided to hang back for a few minutes to see if he could observe anyone around the cabin. His patience paid off five minutes later when he saw a young woman walk outside and light up a cigarette. Young to him, at least. She appeared to be in her early twenties.

She was facing away from him as he quietly walked toward her. He could tell she had quite the hourglass figure. She had long, brown hair and it was hanging over her shoulders. She was wearing a pair of tight Jeans and a red halter-top. The jeans really showed her shape.

When Jay was about fifteen feet away, he said, "Hello."

This startled the girl. She jumped. When she turned and saw him, she smiled sheepishly.

"You scared me."

Jay smiled. "I'm sorry to have scared you."

He walked up to the girl. "My name is Jay."

"I'm Karen. It's nice to meet you," she said. "Where did you come from?"

Jay told her he'd started on Skyline Drive at Milepost 74 and he was heading to Little Run Overlook, where he was then going to cut back down the Drive to get to his truck.

He asked Karen who she was staying with and she told him she was by herself. Jay asked if he could bum a cigarette off her.

"Sure, they are Marlboro Reds, if that's okay."

"That's perfect. That's what I smoke." He inhaled mightily, and as he exhaled, Jay asked her, "Do you normally stay out in the mountains all by yourself?"

"Sometimes I do. I like to get away at times. Sometimes I'll come out here with a friend or two, but more times than not I come out here alone."

The more they talked, the more Jay thought about two things: He really wanted to screw this girl, and he really wanted to slice her throat as well. The thought of blood spurting out of her neck really turned him on. He imagined her eyes, opened wide in terror. Her chest, taking its last few breaths.

He smiled at her and she smiled back. She'd told him she'd been staying at the cabin for three nights and he sensed she was getting a little lonely. She asked him if he wanted a cup of coffee or tea and he told her that tea would be fine.

"Ice tea or hot tea?"

"Ice tea is fine if it's already made."

She pointed to a jug of sun tea that was on the side of the porch. Laughing, she got up and grabbed it, and turned to go into the cabin.

Jay followed her inside. She found two glasses and poured the cups of tea. Jay thanked her as she handed him his cup. He took a drink, thinking about what was going to happen next.

They stood in the small kitchen area, making small talk while drinking their tea. As Jay drained his glass, Karen reached out with her right hand to take his empty glass from him. As she took it, he gently grasped her hand with both of his hands.

Surprised, she jerked her hand away from his, dropping the glass in the process.

"You'd better leave right now," Karen told him as she stepped back.

Jay, knowing that the element of surprise was now gone, said he was sorry and turned to leave. He heard her moving behind him as he stepped towards the door.

As he grasped the doorknob, he turned to look at her. She was standing about five feet away from him with a puzzled look on her face.

"Why did you do that?"

"I'm sorry. I'm not sure what came over me. I just wanted to hold your hands. I didn't mean anything by it."

She hesitated, and then took one step towards him.

In an instant, he pulled his knife and lunged toward her, turning and slicing at the same time. He saw the blade go from one ear to the other. Her look changed to shock, fear and pain in a split second.

She fell, grabbing at him as she did so, but he

stepped away from her. Jay's thoughts were now on how he was going to cover up this one. Mistakes....mistakes, I've made mistakes.

Karen was lying on the floor. Blood was gushing out of her throat. She was gurgling. She was trying to hold her throat, but the blood came through her fingers. Her eyes were on Jay. They were beautiful, wide-eyed and unblinking. Jay turned, pulled a single cigarette out of her pack along with the lighter and walked onto the porch.

Standing there smoking that cigarette, he thought if someone walked up the trail, he would be royally fucked. He'd then have a witness who could place him at the cabin. However, he stood there calmly and smoked the entire cigarette, tossing the butt onto the ground.

As he did so, he knew his DNA would be on that cigarette butt, but he really didn't care. He opened the door and walked inside. Karen was still. Her chest was not moving. Her beautiful green eyes stared at the ceiling like two pieces of colored glass. He could tell Karen was dead.

Damn, what am I going to do now? he thought.

CHAPTER 33

Karen was lying about five feet from the front door of the cabin. There was a growing puddle of blood forming around her. The front of her chest and her halter-top were soaked in blood as well. Her mouth was wide open in a shocked expression and her head was tilted to the side.

Damn, I've really screwed up with this one, Jay thought.

He stood there, his arms crossed, just thinking about what he was going to do next. For some reason, he felt calm. He wasn't even worried, although he knew at this moment he stood his greatest chance of getting caught.

If he was caught and charged with murder, it would be capital murder. Capital murder in the Commonwealth of Virginia would get him the death penalty. Of course, if they found out about all of the other victims, it would ensure he'd get the death penalty. That is, if he didn't get off on an insanity plea.

Knowing all of that, Jay reached down and pulled out another cigarette. He lit it, and stood there smoking it, flicking ashes on Karen's dead body from time to time. By the time he finished the cigarette he had a plan.

The cabin was an old house dating back to the 1800's. It was there before Skyline Drive was ever made into a National Park. Back in the 1930's, when the work for the Shenandoah National Park first started, the residents who lived inside what are now the park boundaries, were basically pushed out of the park.

A few of their homes were now cabins that had been restored and were available to rent. Karen had told him while chatting she was paying $22 a night for the cabin.

Hmm, that's a pretty good price to rent an entire cabin. Jay wondered if that included the pots and pans he saw in the kitchen as well as everything else in the cabin. It had some basic furniture, but nothing too fancy. The wood was old, as was the little bit of furniture that was in the building.

Looking around, Jay found a small lantern that had a 16.4-ounce propane fuel cylinder screwed onto the bottom of it. Now he knew exactly what he was going to do.

* * *

First, he dragged Karen and got her onto the old, worn out couch. He got his hands bloody when he moved her and he left a trail of blood across the floor.

He washed himself in the sink, using plenty of soap to rid himself of the stench of blood. He then went to each window and pulled the curtains shut. He took the blankets off the mattress and put them on the floor in a loose ball, under the wooden framed bed.

The couch had cheap foam cushions with old covers that zipped onto them. He slid them out from under Karen's body. He took the foam cushions out of the covers and put the covers aside.

He found some extra sheets in the closet and he took them out as well. Rolling them into a loose ball as well, he put them under Karen's torso.

With all of that done, Jay picked up Karen's lighter and the lantern. He thought for a second, then sat them down and walked back outside. Using his shirttail, he wiped the doorknob clean of any possible prints he may have left on it.

Looking up and down the trail both ways, Jay didn't see a single person. He hadn't passed any hikers at all since leaving Smith's Run Falls. The later it got in the day, he figured the less chance there would be of anyone starting to hike the trails. Looking at his map, he noticed that Skyline Drive and a parking area did not seem to be that far away.

Jay went back inside and picked up the lantern and lighter again. He unscrewed the propane fuel cylinder from the lantern. He shook it. He could tell it still had plenty of fuel left. He screwed the cylinder back on, but this time, he left it loose where he could hear some of the fuel escaping.

Jay took the lantern and held it so the escaping gas would go into the curtains, the blankets, the sheets, the cushion covers, the mattress and the furniture. He didn't know if the fuel would stay there, but it was worth a try.

Holding the lantern in one hand and the lighter in the other, he lit it. He held the flame close to the area where the fuel was leaking. It almost immediately caught fire.

Jay moved quickly from room to room. He lit every curtain, the pile of sheets under the mattress, the mattress itself, the cushion covers he'd spread out at Karen's head and feet, the sheet under her, the couch itself and finally, he lit the old cushioned chair which he'd pulled close to the front door of the cabin.

The lantern itself was in flames by this time, as were different parts of the cabin. Jay threw the lantern in the flames that was burning where Karen's body was lying. Jay stood there for a few seconds, watching the flames leap up the curtains, tickling the ceiling. Karen's body was now totally engulfed and smoke was quickly filling the small cabin.

As Jay opened the front door to escape, he heard the fire roar from the fresh air coming in the door. Jay pushed the door shut and took off running up the trail.

His hand was burned and he knew he looked and smelled smoky. Jay debated which way to run and he decided to take the long way toward the falls.

However, he stopped running within a minute or so when he heard what he thought were gunshots. He was tempted to turn around and go back to investigate, but then he figured it must be the glass windows bursting.

Jay made it to Oak Tree Falls and quickly stopped to wash both his now-blistering hands and his face. He couldn't see himself, but he hoped that his sweat streaks would hide any smoky traces that were on him.

Jay took off running again and made it back to Smith's Runs Falls without seeing anyone. He was almost back to his vehicle.

Running from the waterfalls back to the parking area, Jay finally heard some sirens. He figured someone must have seen the smoke and contacted either the Fire Department or the Rangers. Looking at his watch, he realized that about thirty minutes had passed since he had first left the cabin. If it was still burning, it had to be burned to the ground by now.

Jay heard voices as he was getting close to the parking area, so he slowed to a walk. He wanted to get his breathing under control before he saw anyone.

Coming into the parking area, he saw a couple talking. They greeted him as he walked by and asked how far he had hiked. Jay, keeping his hands clasped behind his back to hide his blisters, told them to Smith's Run Falls. They then asked him if he was from the area, or had he traveled far to get there. He told them he lived in Maryland.

When they said they were from West Virginia, he figured he was safe. They chatted for another minute, enough time to find out they were heading home this evening. Then Jay told them he had to be getting back home himself.

Pulling out of the parking lot, he saw the couple look in his direction. He waved to them, hoping by doing so they wouldn't look at his license plate or too hard at his truck. They both waved back as he pulled onto the road.

* * *

Driving, his hands resting gingerly on the steering wheel, Jay passed another fire truck with its sirens blasting away, followed by a Ranger vehicle with its lights and sirens on. Jay hoped the cabin had burned down completely. Hopefully, it would make the news by tomorrow so he could hear the extent of the damage.

CHAPTER 34

The ride back to Cutler was long and painful. Jay could see the blisters enlarging on his hands. He was going to have a tough time explaining how he got them.

Should he go home or should he go to Lynn's house? Lynn was probably home from work by now as was Angela. Of course, he had told Angela there was always the possibility that he was going to spend the night in one of the shelters along the Appalachian Trail, so he could probably get away with not going home until tomorrow.

But, if anyone saw his hands and put two and two together, he'd be in trouble. Looking again at them, Jay noticed the blisters were mainly on the insides of his first fingers and thumbs on each hand. He imagined that was from grasping the cylinder.

He only had one blister on the top of his hand.

He decided to stop off at a pharmacy to pick up some salve. He also got a box of band-aids. He got in and out of the pharmacy without anyone giving him more than a cursory glance.

Jay decided to go home and take his chances with Angela. When he finally pulled into his driveway, he was pleasantly surprised to find her car gone. The house was dark and empty. She must have gone somewhere with the kids thinking I wouldn't be home tonight. Good, this will give me a chance to get cleaned up.

Jay went inside and immediately stripped down and turned on the shower. Prior to stepping into the tub, he reached into his pants pocket and pulled out Karen's lighter and his pocketknife. He lit it and held it under the tip of the blade in order to sterilize it.

Using the tip of the knife, which he kept very sharp, he lanced each blister and let the fluid drain out. He really didn't notice any pain at all while doing this. After that was done, he got into the shower and took a long, relaxing shower.

After finishing, he dried off and then took care of his hands. They didn't look as bad now as they did before. He put some of the cream on and then covered them using the band-aids.

He got dressed in a pair of shorts and a t-shirt. He took his dirty clothes downstairs and put them in the washer. He didn't notice any blood at all on his clothes, but they had a strong odor of smoke about them.

Jay was tired, but he wanted to stay up until the clothes were done. Angela might think it a little strange if she got home and found out he was washing the clothes that he'd worn that day. He put the washing machine on the short cycle and his intent was to get the clothes out as soon as they were done and to put them in the dryer on high to dry them as quickly as possible.

Angela didn't get home until after 11. Jay had time to finish washing and drying his clothes and he even folded them up and put them away in his dresser. By the time Angela rolled in, Jay was asleep.

* * *

Jay was up early the next morning. He already had finished one cup of coffee and read the newspaper before Angela came out. She immediately noticed the band-aids on his hands and asked him what happened.

"While I was hiking, it got into my mind to climb a tree. Shit, I don't know why. I hadn't climbed a tree since I was a kid, but I wanted to do it."

"So what happened? You fell?"

"Well, it was pretty easy going up and even coming back down. Until the last eight feet or so. I slipped. It was kind of like when fireman slide down a pole, except I was on a tree and not a smooth pole. The bark tore my hands up."

"Are you okay?" Angela asked.

"I'm fine. I really don't need the band-aids, but

I'm keeping them on just to keep the scrapes clean so I don't risk infection."

They chatted for a few minutes longer while Angela made her cup of coffee. She said she wanted to sit out on the back porch to drink her coffee. Jay got up and went out with her.

They sat in silence for a few minutes. Angela sipped her coffee.

Jay was thinking about the article in today's paper, describing the fire that destroyed a cabin in the Shenandoah National Forest and the fact that a body had been found inside. The article went on to report that Virginia State Police were investing both the cause of the fire and the cause of death. The writer didn't know if the body was that of a male or female, as the VSP wouldn't release any information about the victim until the next of kin had been notified.

Jay was relieved to read the cabin had been destroyed, but he didn't know if all of the evidence had been ruined.

* * *

All of a sudden, Jay remembered something. He'd smoked two cigarettes outside and had thrown both butts on the ground. He'd carelessly thought about this while up there, but he never picked the butts up even though his DNA would be on them.

He hoped the fire had caused the cabin to collapse and the butts were consumed by flames or crushed into the ground by firemen's boots. That way, either they wouldn't be found or the DNA would be unrecoverable.

He probably wouldn't find out more about the investigation for several more days.

"Is everything okay, Jay?"

"Sure, why do you ask?"

"You're staring into space and you haven't said anything for awhile. Have you been listening to me?"

Jay told her he was still waking up and he was just fine. Angela appeared to accept that and she got up, saying she was going to call her mother to check on the kids.

Jay stared into his backyard, vaguely hearing Angela talking on the phone inside the house. He thought about killing Karen yesterday and how simple it had really been. How many was this now?

Jay knew he was going to kill again. It was in his blood. There was no way he could stop and he didn't want to stop. He still hadn't made it to Richmond to kill someone yet. However, the mountains and all of the trails up there were ripe for the pickings. Unless, they came out and said that Karen was murdered. If they said that, everyone would be put on alert.

Today is Saturday. I'm going to kill someone again before next Friday. Whether it's someone in the mountains, over in Richmond or right here around town. It was going to happen and there would be no mistakes with this one.

Angela walked back and said the kids were fine and her mother was going to take them to Busch Gardens for the day. She said she was going to use this as an opportunity to go do some shopping.

"Do you want to come with me?"

"No thanks," Jay mumbled.

She went inside to get ready while Jay sat there thinking.

CHAPTER 35

Dave had been watching Jay for several weeks now. Still, he had no concrete evidence Jay was the killer. His gut feeling was getting stronger. Circumstantial evidence, as weak as it may be, was also pointing to Jay as the culprit.

Dave had received a call from the Virginia State Police a couple of hours ago, about the cabin that had burned in the National Forest. They requested he come to the cabin so he could see first-hand what happened.

He arrived after a forty-minute drive from Cutler. After parking, he hiked down a trail approximately a half-mile. There, the trail forked off and he took a smaller footpath about a hundred yards to where the cabin had been.

Now, the cabin was only smoldering ruins. Only

the stone chimney was still standing. Dave met with the VSP Special Agents upon his arrival at the cabin.

"Hey Dave, thanks for coming," Frank said. Frank Wilson was an ex-Cutler cop who had gone to the VSP five years ago. He was sharp. He had made special agent in two years.

"Not a problem, Frank. Whatcha got here?"

"It appears the body is a female. The medical examiner says it appears her throat was cut. Odds are, that is the cause of death. Until an autopsy is done though, we won't know for sure."

"If her throat was cut, it could be the same person who is doing the killings in Cutler."

They chatted for several more minutes while Frank showed Dave around the cabin site. He pointed out to him the spot where several cigarette butts had been found.

"It may be a long shot, but if the killer smoked any of these cigarettes, we may have his DNA. I'm going to put a rush on it at the lab."

Driving back to Cutler, Dave thought about all of this. He had seen Jay smoking a cigarette after he had shot and killed that one girl. Could one of those butts belong to Jay?

Dave figured he'd get a sample of Jay's DNA to send to the lab for comparison. It wouldn't be hard. He'd find something Jay had been drinking out of. Or, if he saw him smoking a cigarette, he'd try to get the butt.

Dave still hoped that Jay would be proven innocent. They went back a long ways. However,

Jay was a different person now than he was when the two of them had worked patrol together.

Dave had an idea.

* * *

Jay was sitting in Dave's office. Dave had called him yesterday and they set up this appointment. Dave had told him he needed to talk to him about the last shooting. It was routine, he just had a few more questions for him.

"Hey buddy, thanks for coming in on your day off. This won't take but a few minutes. Let me get you a cup of coffee first."

Dave walked out, but was back in two minutes.

"You still drink it black, right? I didn't put anything in it."

"Thanks, this is fine."

Jay spent fifteen minutes or so in Dave's office. The "official" talk only lasted five minutes or so. The last ten minutes had been spent catching each other up on their lives.

"Hey buddy. I have another appointment I have to be getting to. Thanks so much for coming in. My guess is you'll be back to work in a few days."

Both men stood up and shook hands. On his way out the door, Jay tossed his Styrofoam coffee cup into the trashcan.

This is perfect, thought Dave. I hope I'm wrong with this. If not, this may be the evidence I need.

CHAPTER 36

Jay was back to work again after a total of almost two weeks off. He'd had his normal seven-day break and then he missed his four graveyards, due to his paid suspension for the last shooting. He was cleared from that shooting just like he was from the previous two.

Driving around on daylight patrol, Jay was thinking about Karen. He might have screwed up by throwing the cigarette butts down on the ground. If his DNA wasn't found though, he was in the clear once again.

The crackle of the radio broke Jay's thoughts.

"EOC to 77, can you 10-25 Ben Franklin's? They have a female shoplifter detained in the back of the store."

"10-4, I'm responding from Main Street," Jay

replied.

The shoplifter was a forty-year-old female that Jay had dealt with periodically over his sixteen-year career. She was only a few years older than he, but she looked at least twenty years his senior. That's what a lifetime of abusing your body does to you, thought Jay.

When Jay arrived, he met with the manager, who told him he'd watched her put pens and magic markers into her purse. She'd refused to open her purse when he had asked her to, so he had her wait in the back of the store while he called the police.

Jay told the female to show him the contents of her purse and she grudgingly did so. When she opened it, Jay pulled out three packs of pencils, a pack of eight magic markers, several pads and three paintbrushes.

The manager identified all of them as merchandise from his store.

Jay asked the lady if she had a receipt and when she said she did not, he immediately took her into custody.

He remembered her from a shoplifting case a year ago. It was her fifth offense at that time. In Virginia, third offense larceny, no matter what the dollar value is, is automatically a felony. Jay didn't bother to run her criminal history before arresting her. He remembered standing in the courtroom when she was convicted of her fifth offense and sentenced to nine months in jail.

"Didn't spending nine months in jail teach you anything about not stealing?" Jay asked her.

"I didn't spend nine months in jail."

"How long were you locked up?"

"I spent four and a half months in jail."

Jay recalled the jail was overcrowded and typically, inmates got released after pulling half their time if they had good behavior.

"So, I guess four and a half months didn't teach you anything either. You still on probation?"

"Yeah."

"How much time was suspended?"

"I was sentenced to two years, but only had to serve nine months. I guess that means I have a little over a year hanging over me."

"Yep, and I guess you'll get that and probably another couple of years for stealing these pencils and markers. Was it worth it to steal $20 worth of stuff just to go to prison for a few years?"

The female didn't reply. She just sat quietly in the back seat of Jay's cruiser for the rest of the drive to the Police Department.

He spent the next hour taking her in front of the magistrate, where she was held with no bond, and then writing up his report.

Dave walked in just as he was finishing his report up.

* * *

They chatted for a few minutes and he asked Dave if he had anything new on the cases he was working.

"Well, not really. You've probably heard the VSP

are calling the dead body found in the burned up cabin in the mountains a murder. They said the victim had her throat slashed and she was dead prior to the cabin being set on fire."

"Wow, were they able to find any evidence?" Jay asked.

"Very little. They did find several cigarette butts outside the cabin and one came back as having the DNA of the victim, but another one came back with another person's DNA. They don't know who this person is and they are checking the DNA against DNA in the system, but as of yet I haven't heard anything about any possible suspects."

Jay's throat was a little dry. Was it his imagination, or was Dave staring at him? Did Dave suspect him? He gulped as he felt his palms getting sweaty.

The two of them chatted for a few more minutes and then Dave told him he had to get back to work.

"Yeah, and I need to get back out on the street. Take it easy, buddy." Jay said, shaking Dave's hand. He noticed Dave wiped his palm on his pants leg while walking away.

Shit, he thinks it's me. Jay was breathing hard as he walked out the door to his car.

CHAPTER 37

Dave was on the phone with the Chief. He explained to him about the DNA evidence linking Jay to the murder up in the mountains. He knew Jay was tied in with the murders here in Cutler as well. It was just a matter of time until he proved it.

In the meanwhile, the VSP had obtained a murder warrant on Jay. Dave and the other investigators were in their call-out gear and were headed towards Jay's house. Even Eli, with a grim look on his face, was in his SWAT gear and was in the back of the truck with the others.

They weren't going to take any chances. A cop wanted for murder had to be treated with the utmost caution. Cops were some of the best-trained individuals in cover and concealment. They were also excellent shots.

Normally, they would stake a house out first before sending everyone to arrest a suspect. In this case, the VSP had two agents and they were raring to go, so Dave rounded up the others. They were in route and would be there in a few minutes.

* * *

Jay had just pulled into Lynn's driveway when he noticed her looking at him through the window. He waved to her, but she stepped away from the window.

What's with her? Normally, she'd come to the door with a kiss for him. She'd obviously seen him, but here he was halfway to the house and the door was still closed.

He opened the screen door and still she did not come. He knocked on the door and waited about two seconds before opening it.

Lynn was a few feet away from the door. She had a scared look that he hadn't seen before.

"What's wrong, honey?" he asked.

"Jay, I found something today and I want to know what it is."

"What are you talking about?"

"I found a red bio-hazard bag hidden downstairs in the basement. When I opened it, I saw what looks like a pair of gloves with dried blood on them."

Jay's face turned white. When he looked at Lynn, he knew that she suspected something. She was nervous and fidgety. She took a step back.

"Ah, those gloves. I had completely forgotten

about them. I had them on when John shot a deer that had been hit by a car. I helped drag the deer out of the road and I got blood on my gloves. I threw them in that bio-hazard bag and I brought it in your house a while back and then forgot all about it."

"Why were they behind the washing machine?"

"Shit, I had just tossed them on top of the machine. I missed and I meant to get them later on, but I forgot all about it."

Lynn seemed to relax a bit. Jay wasn't sure what she'd been thinking, but she seemed to accept his excuse.

"Just get the damn things out of my basement."

"I'll take them today."

"You better."

Bitch, Jay thought.

They sat around and chatted about a few things, but the conversation was stilted and unnatural. Lynn got up after a bit and said she was going to make them something to eat.

After eating, Jay took a bottle of Coors Light out of the 'fridge. This shit's like water, he thought, but I am trying to cut back on my drinking.

"Hey, Lynn, you don't mind if I drink this beer, do you?"

"No, go ahead, but don't get drunk tonight."

Jay was watching the Orioles game on TV when Lynn said she was going to go straighten up downstairs. Jay barely heard her. He was totally engrossed in the Orioles game as they were battling the Red Sox in a tight one.

About ten minutes later, it hit him. He had also

tossed his backpack downstairs. He forgot, but it was not hidden. In his backpack, he had a bloody knife and another pair of bloody gloves. He also had an eighteen-inch machete in there that he wanted to use sometime.

He was at the basement door when Lynn strode through, holding the machete.

* * *

They had Jay's house surrounded. His truck was not in the driveway. One of the detectives peeked in the garage and said it wasn't there either. They knocked on the door, but no one answered. They tried calling his home number. They could hear the phone ringing, but no one picked up.

They made entry through both the front and back doors. They searched, but Jay was not there.

"Damn, he must not be here. I wonder where he is?"

Dave told the agents he had a girlfriend. If they could find her, he might be with her.

* * *

"What the fuck is this and what is it doing in my house? Jay, what have you been doing? Are you behind some of the killings that have taken place?"

She had a scared look on her face and she was holding the machete, tightly clenched with her arm drawn back.

Shit, it's all over now, Jay thought. Lynn was

going to have to die.

"Honey, what in the world are you so upset about? Put that machete down before you hurt yourself."

"Jay, it's starting to come together for me now. You are involved with some of the recent killings. I know it. Stay away from me. I'm calling 911."

As she picked up the phone, Jay walked toward her. She started to dial 911, when he jumped forward and slammed the phone down. He grabbed at the machete, but she pulled away from him. She yanked her arm back with the machete in hand as if she were going to hit him.

Jay tackled her, trying to pin her arm down as he got close to her. He was able to get her arm pinned to the floor, but she was fighting like crazy. Jay had his left foot on her right arm as he sat on top of her.

He punched her in the face just as she punched him as hard as she could in his groin area.

The pain radiated through Jay's body. He fell backwards and she bucked her body, throwing him off her. She jumped up and came at him, swinging the machete.

Jay saw the blade come down. His shirt tore wide open. He saw the blood before he felt any pain. He fell backwards on the floor. He didn't know how bad she had cut him. However, Lynn looked like she was going to try to slice him again.

Jay rolled over and grabbed a fireplace poker that was lying near him. He chucked it at Lynn, hitting her in the head, causing her to fall backwards.

Jay got up slowly, not seeing where Lynn was. She must have fallen on the other side of the couch.

He was a bit wobbly, but he didn't think the cut was too deep.

He took a deep breath. He was clutching his side where he was bleeding. It hurt like hell. He slowly started to walk towards the couch. All of a sudden, Lynn jumped to her feet from behind the couch holding a small pistol. As Jay recognized what she had in her hand, he yelled at her, "Drop the fucking gun."

At about the time he got the word gun out of his mouth, he saw her raise the gun up chest high. Her finger was on the trigger. She glared at him and he heard her yelling something, but he couldn't understand what she was saying. She pulled the trigger as he was turning away from her. He felt the bullet slam into his body. He went down hard and fast.

* * *

Lynn stood there for a few seconds with the gun pointed right at Jay, but he didn't move. She was shaking as she realized he was the serial killer that they were looking for.

She went to pick up the phone, and she saw where it was broken from where Jay had slammed it. She wasn't getting a dial tone.

She hesitated, but decided to go next door to call the police. She got a glimpse of herself in the mirror as she walked out. She was a mess. She had blood on her face and her eye was starting to get puffy.

She ran next door, but no one was home. She

thought about breaking in, but decided against it and went to the next house. Again, no one was home, so she went to the third house. She told herself that if no one answered at this house, she was going to break in to get to a telephone.

Someone was home and Lynn quickly told the woman that she needed to call the police. The lady, thinking that Lynn's boyfriend must have beaten her, let her come inside to use the phone. However, when she heard Lynn tell the dispatcher that she had just shot and killed the serial killer, she went white.

Lynn told the dispatcher that she was going to stay on the line and wait right where she was until the police got there.

She heard the sirens coming within what seemed like seconds.

CHAPTER 38

"Ma'am, that's correct. We have completely searched your house and there is no one in there. We have put out APB's for him, but at this time we do not know where he is. His truck is not in your driveway. The first officer got here within three minutes after you called 911, so he couldn't have gotten far away. We'll find him."

Lynn sat there, not comprehending what they were saying. What do they mean, he is not in the house. She had shot and killed him. He couldn't have just gotten up and walked out and drove away.

"Ma'am. I need to ask you some questions, okay? After you shot him, did you walk up to check on him?"

"No, I saw the bullet hit him and I saw him fall. He wasn't moving."

"There's a lot of blood in the house, so we know you hit him. There's a trail of blood leading out the door and over to the driveway, where it stops. You may have shot him and he may even be dying, but he wasn't dead when you walked out of that house."

The officer went on to ask her for permission for the police to collect evidence from the house. Of course, she gave it to them.

A second officer came up to her. He was wearing a suit and he said he was Detective Dave Pavano.

He asked her a lot of questions and Lynn told him everything that she could think of. She told him that recently he had been going up into the mountains quite a bit and maybe he was going to go there to hide out.

The detective told her they had alerted all surrounding areas about Jay including the Virginia State Police, the Park Rangers and every city and county in this half of the state.

He was confident that Jay would be found very soon.

However, Lynn was not so sure. She had gotten to know Jay very well and she knew that he had a way of getting himself out of trouble.

"Has anyone been to his house yet to see his wife and kids?" she asked.

"Well, we were actually there looking for Jay when the call came out that you had shot him here. There are still two officers who are there, just in case he goes home."

"He's going to try to get me again. I just know it. Can't you keep two officers here with me until he's caught?"

"Sure, I'll make sure at least two stay here with you. Don't worry, we are going to find him real soon."

Lynn sat there, wondering when they'd catch Jay. She was still in her neighbor's house while the police were still collecting evidence from her house. She really didn't want to go back into her house until it was cleaned up and Jay was caught. Her neighbor gave her a glass of ice tea and told Lynn she could stay here as long as she needed to.

Lynn thanked her, but told her she would only stay until the police were finished in her house. They sat and talked for a few minutes, but Lynn really wasn't in the mood for talking, so she stopped and just sat there drinking her tea.

Detective Pavano came in after about forty-five minutes. He told her they had searched Jay's house. The search revealed Jay's gun cabinet was empty. Dave knew Jay had plenty of weapons and he knew that Jay knew how to use them all.

Dave wondered where Jay would have gone to and the only thing he could think of was the mountains. He called again, requesting that the Rangers be put on high alert. He told his desk officer to email a color picture of both Jay and the type of truck he owned to every ranger station in the area.

A BOL, Be-On-The-Lookout, went out nationwide with a description of both Jay and his truck. Odds are, if Jay wasn't picked up very soon, America's Most Wanted would probably be knocking on their door asking if they could profile Jay. It wasn't often that a cop went bad like this and the media was sure to eat it up.

Dave had a lot of work to do as well. He was in shock that one of his best buddies on the force had turned out to be the crazy killer he'd been tracking for these many months. He knew Jay was behind the other homicides. He just had to tie it all together.

Shocking is what it was. Just plain shocking that a good cop like Jay could have killed all of those people.

"I wonder how many more he killed that we don't know about yet?" Dave asked out loud to no one in particular.

CHAPTER 39

Lynn looked in the mirror, admiring her appearance in full dress uniform. She had graduated from the Central Shenandoah Criminal Justice Training Academy just a few hours ago and had just gotten back home.

Her parents had flown down for the ceremony. They had taken her out to dinner after the graduation and now had come back to her house for a few drinks and some catching up. Jay's name had not come up yet, but Lynn knew it would.

Thinking back, it still amazed her that after experiencing the evil that Jay had about him, she had the strength to become a police officer right here in Cutler. She was aware the entire PD knew about her fling with Jay, but she was going to show them all that she was going to be the best police officer ever.

"Honey, come back out. We want to take a few more pictures before you get changed," her mother called to her.

"I'll be right there."

Lynn stood for another minute looking at her reflection. She thought she looked a lot older and more serious than she did just one year ago. I guess getting involved with a serial killer can do that to a person, she thought.

Lynn spent the rest of the day with her parents, just hanging out around her house and talking. They had a late night snack and went to bed around midnight. Her parents had to get up early for a 9AM flight back home.

The send-off went well at the airport and Lynn stood at the window watching the airplane taxi down the runway. As the plane took off, she wondered what her future held for her.

* * *

By the time Lynn got herself some lunch and made it back home, it was after 1PM. The mailman was just pulling away when Lynn pulled up. Getting out of her vehicle, Lynn smiled. It was a beautiful summer day, the grass was green, the flowers blooming and she was now a police officer. Her FTO, Field Training Officer, period of eight weeks would start in three days, but until then, she was off.

She walked to her mailbox and pulled out the normal assortment of junk mail, flyers, one magazine and a letter. The letter had no return address on it. It caught her attention as the handwriting on it looked familiar, but she couldn't quite place it. She also noticed the postmark was from Mexico.

She walked into her house and opened up the letter. She was shaking. It was handwritten.

> I know that you are a police officer. So am I. I will be back and I will finish off what I didn't finish last time. No matter where you go, or what you do, think about me. I may not be there, but then again, I may. When you least expect to see me, I'm going to show up. Go ahead and take this letter to Dave to have him analyze my handwriting and to check for fingerprints. What's that going to prove? Screw him. He couldn't catch me last year and he sure as hell ain't coming down here to try to track me down now. But let him know, he's on my hit list as well. Take care, baby, and watch your back.
>
> Stay Safe,
> Jay

About the Author

Mark Kearney served in the United States Navy, active duty, as an electronics technician from 1987 to 1996. He is currently an ETC (E-7) in the United States Naval Reserves, IRR. He was stationed at 3 major duty stations and several smaller ones for schools. The major ones were in the country of Panama for 2 ½ years, Puerto Rico for 3 years and the state of Maine for 2 ½ years.

As a police officer, Kearney has received several awards. Two were performance commendations, Police Officer of the Year for 2004, distinguished service commendation and good conduct. He has been a police officer for 9 years.

Kearney is one of the co-founders of the Book 'Em event. He is the President of The Book 'Em Foundation and is currently working on spreading the Book 'Em event globally.

Other programs he founded include the "BE a Reader, Cops in Schools Reading Program." He will be spreading this program globally as well. Kearney started a book distribution program in the local schools and by June 2007, he will have handed out over 8,000 free books to students and adults.

He is the only police officer, to his knowledge, to go inside of prisons to talk to groups of prisoners about how they can help themselves while locked up through reading and education.

Kearney has been married for 17 years and has two children. He currently resides in Staunton, VA.

Printed in the United States
99822LV00002B/178-225/A

9 780979 499821